S0-BHV-089

PRISONER OF A PASSIONATE SENORITA

As Captain Gringo's throbbing head cleared he opened his eyes and saw a nice-looking but hard-eyed Spanish Creole dame standing over him. A big moon-faced mestizo loomed behind her, holding a Mauser pistol. That seemed needlessly dramatic—for Captain Gringo's wrists and ankles were lashed to the brass rails of the bedstead.

The woman slapped his face hard and demanded, "Who are you working for, the Cabrera faction or the Barrios family?"

"Never heard of either bunch," the American said.

She slapped him again, smiling coldly at him. Then she said to her big sidekick: "I work better when friends are not watching, Paco."

When she and Gringo were alone, the woman unfastened his belt and pulled his pants down and settled herself on top of him. "Which side are you working for?" she repeated. "If you do not tell me, Yanqui, it will go hard with you!"

Captain Gringo only smiled....

Novels by
Ramsay Thorne

Published by
WARNER BOOKS

ATTENTION: SCHOOLS AND CORPORATIONS

WARNER books are available at quantity discounts with bulk purchase for educational, business, or sales promotional use. For information, please write to: SPECIAL SALES DEPARTMENT, WARNER BOOKS, 666 FIFTH AVENUE, NEW YORK, N.Y. 10103.

**ARE THERE WARNER BOOKS
YOU WANT BUT CANNOT FIND IN YOUR LOCAL STORES?**

You can get any WARNER BOOKS title in print. Simply send title and retail price, plus 50¢ per order and 50¢ per copy to cover mailing and handling costs for each book desired. New York State and California residents add applicable sales tax. Enclose check or money order only, no cash please, to: WARNER BOOKS, P.O. BOX 690, NEW YORK, N.Y. 10019.

Renegade #24

GUATEMALA GUNMAN

Ramsay Thorne

WARNER BOOKS

A Warner Communications Company

WARNER BOOKS EDITION

Copyright © 1984 *by Lou Cameron*
All rights reserved.

Warner Books, Inc.
666 Fifth Avenue
New York, N.Y. 10103

 A Warner Communications Company

Printed in the United States of America

First Warner Books Printing: *May, 1984*

10 9 8 7 6 5 4 3 2 1

Renegade #24
GUATEMALA GUNMAN

Guatemala City seemed a nice enough place for a short visit, but Captain Gringo didn't think he'd want to die there. So by the time a distant church bell warned him la siesta would soon be over, the tall, blond, wanted man was pacing his hotel rug and muttering nasty things about his sidekick, Gaston.

The plan had called for Captain Gringo to lie low in their hotel suite a discreet distance from police headquarters while the less conspicuous member of the team scouted the railroad depot and, with any luck, picked up a couple of tickets to the coast.

The two soldiers of fortune had completed the mission that brought them to Guatemala in the first place. And they'd even been paid off, for a change. So now it was time to vamoose before anyone important got around to asking what they were doing in the country without the permission or, hopefully, the knowledge of the current government.

Gaston had suggested and Captain Gringo had agreed that the best time to make their way out of town would be smack in the middle of la siesta, when even cops who read reward posters would be goldbricking. But unless both that church bell and Captain Gringo's pocket watch were wrong, la siesta was almost over, and Gaston had promised to get back before it started!

The tall American moved out to the balcony of their second-story corner suite to see if there was any sign of his often unpredictable little pal. He didn't see Gaston or anyone else on the steep cobbled calle running down toward the main drag. La siesta had a few minutes to go. So the view across the rooftops belied the facts of life in Guatemala this season.

The country was beset by natural and political disasters that figured to get worse before they got better. But everything in sight looked serene and static as a picture postcard printed in colors a bit too bright to be real.

Guatemala City was well watered as well as cooled by the trade winds climbing the slopes from the northeast. So all the treetops were a bright Kelly green. The rooftops between seemed to be tiled with tangerine peels, and at some time in the past Guatemala City had gotten a real buy on some wild paint. Most of the stucco walls in sight were flamingo pink. Those few decorated by freethinkers tended to be lavender or powder blue. All the exposed wooden trim, however, was the same shade of electric blue. It was supposed to keep the flies and mosquitoes out. It didn't, but what the hell.

Captain Gringo consulted his watch again as he considered the possible ways a dirty old man could wind up late from school. How long was a guy with common sense supposed to wait for another who'd either met up with an old drinking buddy, a new dame, or the law? If Gaston had been picked up, leaving right now might not be soon enough!

But it was a quarter to three. So in fifteen minutes the streets would start to clutter up with all sorts of people, and other people had posted reward posters on him in all sorts of places! He had money and a few extra rounds for the .38 riding in its shoulder rig under his linen jacket. After that, it got complicated.

The erstwhile Dick Walker of the U.S. Tenth Cav wasn't called Captain Gringo because he looked like a native down here. He'd learned the hard way that there were local boys who'd give an obvious Yanqui a hard time even if they *hadn't* seen his face on a reward poster. But if Gaston had been picked up, it wasn't safe to wait until dark to make his move, and if Gaston had been picked up trying for a couple of lousy railroad tickets, where was there to run to?

Legging it cross-country through terrain he didn't know sounded almost as risky as staying put and hoping Gaston was just jerking off somewhere. But *almost* as risky wasn't as risky as waiting to find out after it was too late to run.

He put his watch away and muttered, "Okay, we'll give him until five to three. That'll give us time to get at least a couple of blocks away before anyone here spots us leaving without checking out."

He was still trying to decide the direction of his planned evacuation when he heard a gentle rapping on the chamber door inside. He didn't think it could be a raven. It wasn't Gaston's knock. That left a chambermaid or a cop.

He didn't want to shoot or even scare a chambermaid. So he put his hand inside his jacket but didn't draw his .38 as he stepped back inside to call out, "Quién es?" while starting across the rug to the door.

He didn't make it. Some son of a bitch who'd been lying

for him just inside the balcony door dropped an office safe on his head, and the world exploded in clouds of black ink and little pinwheeling stars as he fell ass over teakettle into a seemingly bottomless pit for a thousand miles and a million years.

Floating forever like a jellyfish in a sea of spit-warm ink wouldn't have been so bad if it hadn't smelled so awful. Captain Gringo sneezed and tried to turn his face away from the gagging reek of violets and ammonia. But some dumb dame kept shoving the smelling salts under his nose and telling him he was just fine. So he opened his eyes to tell her she was full of shit.

She laughed. He didn't see what was so funny. As his throbbing head began to clear enough to matter, he saw she was a nice-looking but hard-eyed Spanish Creole, apparently dressed for a funeral. The big moon-faced mestizo looming behind her was dressed in black, too. He was covering Captain Gringo with a Mauser pistol. That seemed needlessly dramatic when Captain Gringo tried to move and couldn't. They'd placed him on his own bed after knocking him out. His wrists and ankles were lashed to the brass rails at the head and foot of the heavy bedstead. The spooky brunette was seated atop the covers with him. Her hip was against his rib cage and she held a carpetbag in her lap. As she put the smelling salts away in it, he noticed the gleam of nickel plate and knew where his .38 had gone as well.

She closed the snap of her bag and said, "Bueno. To save the usual fencing, your compañero, Gaston Verrier, is not coming back to rescue you, Captain Gringo. We are holding him in another part of town. As you see, you are completely in my power."

Captain Gringo tested the slack in the látigo thongs holding his wrists above his head as he grimaced and said, "When you're right you're right. You sure suckered me good with that old chestnut. Let's see if I've got it right. You sent your tame ape, there, in through Gaston's adjoining room so I wouldn't hear him pick the cheap hotel lock. Then you tapped coy as hell on the other door and . . ."

She slapped his face hard and snapped, "*We* shall ask all the questions here, Captain Gringo! To begin with, who are you working for, the Cabrera faction or the Barrios family?"

He frowned up at her and replied, "Neither. Never heard of either bunch."

She slapped him again. He called her a stupid cunt in English before repeating, in Spanish, "Señorita, I don't know who in the hell you're talking about. Gaston and me didn't come up here to mix in local politics. We were hired by an international insurance company to locate a client they were worried about. We found her, dead. We came here to report to them. They were happy to know they didn't have to pay off a double-indemnity policy, so we all parted friends."

Her eyes were cold as she smiled down at him and told her mooselike sidekick to wait in the next room, adding, "I work better when friends are not watching, Paco."

Paco, if that was his name, said, "The Yanqui is very big, and they say he is very tough, Señora Pantera!"

But the panther lady, if that was *her* name, insisted she wanted to be alone with Captain Gringo. So in a very few moments they were.

Neither said anything for a time as they studied each other. He wasn't too inspired by his view. The dame was pretty enough, save for a faint mustache and the way her eyebrows sort of met in the middle above those cold dark eyes. She placed the carpetbag on his chest and rose to fork one leg over his, lifting her long skirt daintily to do so. She lifted it high enough for him to notice, over the top of the bag, that she wasn't wearing anything under it. She sure was hairy as hell down there, too.

Not knowing what to say, Captain Gringo simply watched, bemused, as the weird woman unfastened his belt and pulled his pants down between her naked thighs before moving up on the bed to settle her open groin teasingly close to his own exposed privates. She stared down thoughtfully and said, "I see you are still soft. Don't you think I'm pretty?"

He grinned up at her wryly and replied, "I think you're loco en la cabeza, too. But if this is your idea of refined torture, I'm game."

She repeated, "Which side are you working for?" as she unsnapped the carpetbag between them again and reached inside, adding, "I must warn you that if your story does not match that of your friend, Gaston, it will go hard with you."

He tried to shrug but couldn't as he said, "It's already starting to get hard. But I don't know what you're talking about, Doll. The only Guatemalan rebel faction we ever heard about was some nut called Caballero Blanco, and he's dead. Those other names don't mean a thing to me."

She took out a jar, opened it, and began to smear his dawning erection with the contents as she purred, "You will have to do better than that."

Her skilled hands felt great as they slithered up and down his shaft. But the grease she was rubbing on it had to go! He winced and said, "Jesus H. Christ! What the hell are you using for lubrication, doll?"

She said, "Oil of eucalyptus with red pepper juice. Does it burn?"

"You can say that again! It feels like my pecker's on fire, and I *still* don't know anyone up here named Barrios or Cabrera, you bitch!"

She inched her bared vagina closer to his now-throbbing erection as she insisted, "Of course you do. You have to be working for one or the other. So tell me, and maybe we can be *friends,* eh? Would you like to have it in me, Captain Gringo? I would like very much for to take your nice big thing inside me to the roots, but if you persist in being so uncooperative..."

"Honey, you've no idea how cooperative I feel right now! Could you, ah, stroke it some more?"

She laughed coyly and said, "Oh no, we would not wish for you to have an orgasm just yet. But, as you see, the hot salve keeps it most hard, no matter how else we stimulate it. I'll bet you could come right now with one or two strokes, no?"

"I sure could. Listen, why don't you go back to just smacking me in the face a lot, Pantera? I think that might confuse a guy less."

She purred, "I am sure it would," as she moved the bag aside to give him a better view. She reached down between them and began to play with her own privates as she observed, calmly enough, considering, "You are well known all over Central America as a man who machine-guns people for money. Naturally, you were recruited to come here and work for one side or the other during the current crisis. Nobody but the Cabreras or the Barrios have the money it would take to hire such expensive outside help. Surely you can see that, Captain Gringo?"

"That's not all I can see! You're not rubbing that hot salve on your own clit, are you, Pantera?"

"Sí; it feels most stimulating. If you would only be a good

boy I would show you how nice it feels for to screw a woman with eucalyptus oil all over everything! It feels hot and spicy going in. Cold and minty coming out. Would you like for to shove it in and out of me very fast, Querido?''

''Right now I'd be willing to screw a busted bottle! It's driving me crazy!''

''It's supposed to. Tell me who hired you and we can come together. I confess I feel most stimulated myself now. But you can't have me until you tell me all you know!''

''What happens then? You leave me here with hot grease on my dong and a bullet in my brain?''

''Perhaps, but don't you wish to enjoy the orgasm of your life before you die? Why are you teasing us both this way, you naughty boy? You know you will tell me sooner or later. So why not make it sooner, and perhaps I will let you come in me *twice* before I . . . leave.''

He tried to shrug again. He noticed she paid no attention to the way he moved his bound wrists. She was breathing sort of funny as she strummed her old banjo, and if only he could gain some time . . .

He said, ''Look, I don't know the details. But that one name, Barrios, rings a bell.''

''Aha! So you are working for *those* stuck-up bastards, eh?''

''I'm not sure. We were recruited by a guy called Klondike. A Yank, like me. Ever hear of him?''

''No. Should I have?''

''Guess not. Suffice it to say he's a well-known knock-around guy down here. You can check that out if you like.''

He knew she couldn't, even as he saw that she was making a mental note on a guy Captain Gringo knew for sure was dead, having shot the son of a bitch himself. She inched even closer, so that his turgid shaft was pressed between the open lips of her own greased opening as she moved her aroused clit up and down it, asking, "Which of the Barrios brothers did this Klondike say you'd be working for?"

"There are brothers?" he replied, as he tried to move enough to satisfy his own tortured flesh. She let him, enjoying his frustration, as she said, "Do not play games with me, Querido. You know there are many Barrios in Guatemala. I must know which of them saw fit to hire a private machine-gun crew."

He started thrusting frantically with his hips as she rode him cruelly, obviously enjoying what he was doing for her teasing clit while she left him out in the cold. He knew a dame could come that way. He knew a dame ready to come might not be paying much attention to anything else a guy might be up to. So he made his move.

Pantera tried to scream as the hand he'd worked loose from the látigo thongs whipped down to grab her by the nape of the neck. But Captain Gringo's hand was big enough to work a thumb into her voice box before she could call for help. So the struggle was silent, savage, and sort of interesting toward the end.

As he choked her unconscious, Pantera tried to rise from the bed but succeeded only in moving up a bit as, either accidentally or in an attempt to make friends in a hurry, she settled down on his shaft to the roots.

She was right about how wild it felt, he saw, as her convulsions moved her overspiced interior up and down his raging erection. He came in her, hard, and might have done so again had she not suddenly gone limp and just lain there atop him. It still felt great, but with a guy in the next room about to bust in any minute with a Mauser, he had more important things than sex on his mind.

He rolled the unconscious Pantera off him and fumbled the

.38 out of her open bag on the bed before he risked going to work on the thongs binding his other wrist. The knot was a pisser, or he'd have had *two* hands to choke the bitch with. But he got loose at last, topside, and bent to untie his ankles, with the .38 on the bedspread between them.

He got one leg free. Then the door started to open. He grabbed for his .38 as a familiar face appeared in the doorway. He gasped. "Jesus H. Christ, Gaston! What are *you* doing here? I almost shot you just now!"

Gaston nodded and said, "So I noticed. The species of mestizo you were no doubt expecting was très slow of reflex when I walked in on him just now. Who is your lady friend on the floor, Dick?"

"Just cover her while I untie my ankle, dammit. I don't know what the fuck's going on here, either. Is her pal next door likely to come to in the near future?"

"Merde alors, when I use my knife, they never come to," said Gaston, moving over to stand above Pantera as he reached for his own .38. The girl on the floor moaned and opened her eyes. She blanched as she saw Gaston looming over her. Although, in truth, Gaston didn't loom nearly as much as most men.

The old Legion deserter was one of those small gray men who, at first glance, don't seem to rate a second glance. But both men and women dismissed Gaston at their own peril, for he was as deadly as a cobra and as horny as a billy goat. He was stronger than he looked and could move like spit on a hot stove. So, many a man and more than one woman had wound up dead, or laid, before they'd known what had hit them.

Captain Gringo rolled off the bed and ran for the adjoining bathroom as he held his .38 in one hand and his sagging pants in the other. Pantera propped herself up on one elbow to rub her own overstimulated crotch with her free hand as she stared up at Gaston and said, "I do not understand. My friends were supposed to pick you up at the railroad depot, Señor Verrier."

Gaston smiled down at her and replied, "Merci; I was *wondering* who I was playing tag with during la siesta. The intended ambush at the depot was très league of the bush. But the idiots would persist in following me as I beat my hasty mais discreet retreat. Naturally, I did not consider it wise to come back here to the hotel until I had taken care of them, one by one, in various alleyways of your beautiful city."

She gasped and cried out, "No! You *couldn't* have killed poor Pepe and Quico!"

Gaston shrugged and said, "Keep your voice down. If those were the names of the idiots unwise enough to follow a grown man down an alley, you may rest assured they will never do such a stupid thing again."

She sat up straighter to stare past Gaston through the open door behind him. She spotted Paco's limp left hand on the carpet of the next room and screamed. So Gaston kicked her under the ear to put her back to sleep again. Captain Gringo charged out of the bathroom with his pants refastened but his .38 still in hand and snapped, "Keep it down to a roar in here, for God's sake! They must have heard that yell all over the place!"

Gaston said, "Oui. May one suggest the hauling of our adorable derrieres, tout de suite?"

Since Gaston was already moving for the hallway and neither had checked in with any luggage, Captain Gringo followed, holstering his pistol as they got outside. As they went down the stairwell he told Gaston, "I wanted to *talk* to that dame, dammit! We still don't know who's after us!"

Before Gaston could answer, a hotel porter came around a

bend in the stairs to meet them. He shouted, "I heard a woman scream, señores! What is going on up there?"

Captain Gringo said, "Lovers' quarrel. You'd better get the police. The lady doing all the screaming is waving a knife!"

It worked. The porter turned and ran down the stairs ahead of them, shouting to someone below to call the law. The two soldiers of fortune slowed down as they reached the lobby and simply walked through the confused crowd of hotel guests and help as they all waved their hands and yelled at one another.

Out on the street, some other nosy types were running toward the hotel entrance. They made it to the corner before a khaki-clad cop coming the other way waved them down to ask what was going on. Gaston shrugged and said, "Quién sabe? We heard something about a crime of passion back at that hotel we just passed. Be careful, amigo. They said something about an armed and dangerous woman, so . . ."

That worked, too. The cop dashed past them for the hotel entrance, drawing his .45 on the run. Gaston chuckled and led Captain Gringo around the corner. As they headed uphill, the taller American sighed and said, "Great. Walk don't run to the nearest exit, and it's broad-ass daylight! Are we going anywhere in particular, Gaston?"

Gaston said, "Oui, away from the center of town. By now other species of annoying youths in uniform will have found the cadavers I was forced to leave in various alleyways down the slope. I see yet another alleyway just ahead. May I suggest a stroll in the shade?"

Captain Gringo shook his head and said, "Keep walking straight-arrow. We're too close to the hotel to duck into alleyways with every old biddy within earshot hanging out her window to see what's going on. You know this town better than me, Gaston. How far are we from the city limits? I see some trees on the crest of this rise ahead.''

Gaston said, ''They are only shade trees along a fashionable avenue along the crest, alas. There is more to Guatemala City than meets the eye, Dick. There is a considerable favilla running down the far side of this très fatigué hillside. Poor people, of course, live where the trade winds do not blow through the shutters on a hot day, hein?''

Captain Gringo moved up and on in silence for a moment as he digested that. Then he said, ''Nix on walking into a slum in broad daylight, dressed respectable. What happens if we swing right or left when he hit the fancy-pants avenue ahead?''

''I suggest we swing right. I know some people up that way. At least, I *hope* I do. It has been a long time since I was through here last.''

Captain Gringo asked him how long ago that had been, and Gaston said, ''Almost ten years. But if they do not remember me fondly, they have no sense of gratitude. I served old Justo Barrios well as an artillery officer and—''

''Hold it!'' Captain Gringo cut in, slowing down considerably as he added, ''That dame back there wanted to know whether we'd been hired by some guys named Barrios or, let me think, Cabrera?''

Gaston frowned and said, ''I thought those people were insane, Dick. Are you sure you have the names right?''

''Pretty sure. I was trying like hell to make up a good story while she was smearing the damnedest stuff on my dong. She said she'd been sent to find out if we were working for the Barrios or the Cabrera gang and . . . Who the fuck are we talking about, Gaston?''

They'd reached the crest of the hill by now, and, as Gaston had said, the avenue running along the crest was wide and tree-lined. They looked back down the slope, saw nobody coming up it after them, and headed north as Gaston spotted a sidewalk cantina ahead and suggested they consider the situation over a couple of cooling drinks.

Captain Gringo said, "Are you crazy? We've got to get under cover poco tiempo, Gaston!"

But Gaston insisted he was thirsty and added, "Sometimes the best cover is out in the open, looking innocent. Nobody saw us doing anything exciting back at the hotel, and the police will no doubt slap that silly woman silly for a while before they get around to checking her story, if she tells them any story about us at all, hein?"

Captain Gringo nodded thoughtfully and they cut across the street to the cantina. But he was still on edge and keeping an eye on the corner they'd just rounded as Gaston told the ugly waitress she was beautiful and ordered them some gin and tonics. He waited until they'd been served and it was safe to chat before he explained, "We may have to reconsider approaching my old comrades of the Barrios faction if that species of bitch made any sense at all. When I was here in the noisy eighties, the Barrios and Cabrera clans were on the *same side*!"

Captain Gringo sipped some gin and tonic, reached in his jacket for a smoke, and said, "Tell me about 'em. What's the score here in Guatemala?"

"I wish I knew. As I said, I was hired by one Justo Rufino Barrios, the strong man at the time, to fire field guns at his enemies."

"Were any of 'em named Cabrera?"

"Mais non; we were at war with the combined armies of Nicaragua, El Salvador, and Costa Rica. You know how strong men are."

"He sounds like a popular guy. Where do the Cabrera guys come in?"

"My commanding officer was a Cabrera. Almost all the high-ranking officers were either Cabreras or Barrios. You see, the two extended families run this country. Or at least they did when I served a hitch in their army."

Gaston took out his own Havana claro and lit up before he went on. "One might call it an unholy alliance. The two families worked together to get rid of the Spanish, back in the twenties. Since then, they've been running the so-called republic together. They need each other. Alone, neither clan could rule the roost as well."

Captain Gringo blew a thoughtful smoke ring and asked why.

Gaston said, "The Barrios clan was founded in the days of the Spanish empire by highborn Creole hidalgos. They tend to lisp like Castilians and send their children to Europe to be educated. The late El Presidente Justino Barrios was one of those velvet-glove species of strong man, albeit a bit inclined to be a très annoying neighbor. He encouraged foreign investment, and built schools, hospitals, opera houses, and so forth. He paid *artillery*men quite well, too."

Captain Gringo said, "I get the picture. Tell me about the other bunch."

Gaston said, "The Cabreras are an even larger clan. As peones they naturally tended to have more children in the days of Spanish rule. They don't speak fancy Spanish, and most of them have more than a little Indian blood. They are what you Yanks call good ol' boys, hein?"

Captain Gringo frowned and said, "Then I don't see how they could have much use for one another."

Gaston shrugged and said, "You have a lot to learn about Latin American politics, then. Alone, the aristocratic Barrios family would be faced with constant rebellions. To the average hardscrabble peon, a blanco with a high and mighty Castilian manner is a hated Spaniard. But when the local chief of police is a mestizo who belches and farts as loud as you . . ."

"Gotcha," Captain Gringo cut in, adding, "I can see how having the rougher Cabreras running things at the local level works to the advantage of the ritsy-titsy Barrios clan. But what do the Cabreras get out of the deal?"

"Solvency, of course. Despite their ruder manners, the Cabreras are not fools. They would not wish for it to get around, but some of them have sent *their* sons to school, too."

Gaston sipped some more gin and tonic before he continued. "The powers that be prefer to deal with thugs they consider gentlemen. So, with the so-called presidente usually and the diplomatic corps always Barrios, Guatemala has more foreign investment than the average banana republic. They also have an alarming national debt, but who is going to question the credit of a Castilian gentleman who leaves his napkin in his lap and uses the right fork, hein?"

"I get the picture. As long as the two families work together, they have the best of both worlds. Roughnecks to police the backwoods and smoothies to con the bankers. But how do we know the two gangs are still working together, Gaston?"

Gaston sighed and said, "Merde alors, that is why we are sitting here drinking gin and tonic instead of pounding on the door of my old commanding officer, Colonel Barrios. El Presidente Barrios managed to get himself killed in that combined war with three neighbors in the eighties, but thanks to my très formidable skills with field guns, my own old outfit made it back with modest casualties."

He took another sip from his glass before observing, "If my old CO is still at the same address, and still in a position of power, we should be safe enough in his hands. But if that woman at the hotel was correct in assuming the two clans have had a falling-out . . ."

Captain Gringo frowned thoughtfully and said, "Try it this way. Those people trying to question us wouldn't have had any questions to ask if whatever's supposed to start had already started. That means someone, on one side or the other, is still plotting and hasn't made any serious move yet, right?"

Gaston snorted in disgust and said, "Merde alors, Dick, tell me something I have yet to consider. Obviously some sort of power play is about to transpire. Just as obviously, it would not be at all discreet for us to choose either side until we had some idea which one is most likely to *win!*"

Captain Gringo shrugged and said, "We can't just sit here waiting to find out, dammit! Some cops could come around that corner back there any minute. I vote we look up your old army buddy. I'm surprised you never mentioned you had friends in town."

Gaston grimaced and said, "If I had thought I had friends in town, I would never have risked my adorable ass down by the railroad depot. I said I *knew* Colonel Barrios, Dick. I never said I *trusted* him!"

They were still debating the odds when Gaston pointed out a pink-walled casa that looked more like a fortress than a family home and said, "That is Colonel Barrios's place, one hopes. I still think our best chance would be the railroad depot, after dark. The people who were after us could not have been police, and now that we have more or less eliminated them . . ."

"Dammit," Captain Gringo cut in. "The dame's still alive, and so's the son of a bitch who sent her and those thugs after us! You said yourself that this colonel of yours is too rich to be tempted by the rewards on us, and, what the hell, he *owes* you, right?"

"It was a long time ago and he is not *my* colonel, Dick. He could be the property of our mysterious questioners, non?"

"No. That won't work. The dame damn near killed me trying to find out if we were working for anyone named Barrios, remember?"

"Ah, oui, nobody named Barrios would have to tease your adorable dong to find out if they knew you or not. But doesn't that let the Cabreras off the hook as well?"

"Sure. If we'd been hired by anyone named Cabrera they'd know it. Pantera had to be working for some *other* gang. Let's go tell the Barrios guys."

He started forward. But Gaston grabbed his arm and said, "Wait. I just thought of something. If the two clans have had a falling-out, my money is on the Cabreras! There are more of them and they control the countryside."

"Okay, who do we know named Cabrera?"

"Here in Guatemala City? It was a long time ago, Dick."

"Yeah. Meanwhile we gotta get off the street poco tiempo. Any old port in a storm is better than wandering around out here in the open until we're picked up by God knows who!"

Gaston said he was sure they were getting themselves killed as he led Captain Gringo to the massive oak door and politely pounded the big wrought-iron knocker.

A million years went by and then an old guy who looked like an Egyptian mummy in a butler's outfit opened the door and asked for their calling cards. Gaston explained that they didn't have any calling cards and asked if the colonel was receiving anyway.

The old butler blinked in surprise and stammered, "Colonel Roberto has been dead for almost a year, Señores! Surely you must have heard?"

Captain Gringo swore under his breath as Gaston shook his head and said, "We have been out of the country. Please excuse our distressing gaffe. We are sorry to have disturbed you."

But before they could turn away, the old butler said, "Un momento, por favor! Are you not that French artillery officer who saved the colonel's life in eighty-five, Señor?"

Gaston nodded modestly, and the old man said, "I thought I recognized you! Come in! Come in! I am sure la Señora Barrios will wish for to receive you caballeros!"

Anything beat standing in the street. So they followed the butler inside and across an overgrown patio as Captain Gringo murmured, in English, "What's the story on the ifeway?"

Gaston replied, "I've never met her. I didn't even know he had one. But of course, most homebodies do, hein?"

The butler ushered them into an imposing drawing room and seated them before a baronial albeit cold fireplace. Then he clapped his hands and told the maid, who appeared from nowhere, to fetch them some refreshments while he went to announce them to la señora.

A silver tea service and the widow Barrios showed up at about the same time. The two soldiers of fortune stood up to greet her politely and forgot all about the view down the front of the serving maid's bodice. The lady of the house was some dish indeed.

She was naturally wearing widow's weeds that must have cost her a bundle. A black lace mantilla, draped over a high ebony comb in her light brown hair, framed her heart-shaped face becomingly. Her cameo features were a bit more Latin than her hair. But she was obviously pure blanco. Her black satin dress was cut modestly enough, but she filled it in a way that made her serving maid's scantier costume look downright uninteresting. She smiled sweetly at the maid, who let go of the tea tray and vanished as their hostess said, "Mi casa es su casa, Caballeros! Which one of you was the hero who saved my late husband's life in battle?"

Gaston stammered a modest reply and with no further ado she came over to kiss him fondly. All Captain Gringo got was a hand to kiss. But she sat them both down and poured as she insisted they tell her how she could be of service to them.

Captain Gringo didn't think she could mean that the way a guy in his condition might take it. He'd washed off most of the eucalyptus oil back at the hotel, but his pecker still itched like hell and it didn't help at all to stare at such a spicy-looking little broad.

He shifted his weight gingerly in his seat and, though he knew it was polite to drink some tea first, got right to the point. He said, "We came to warn, ah, your late husband's family, Señora ah . . . ?"

"I am called Evita by my friends, Señor . . . ?"

"I'm Dick Walker. This is Gaston Verrier, of course. I'm sorry to put it so bluntly, but word has gotten out about the pending feud between the Barrios and Cabrera factions."

She went on pouring, with a puzzled little frown, as she said, "That is not possible, Dick. Forgive me. I mean no disrespect, but you have been misinformed. God knows our poor country is having enough trouble at the moment, between the recent volcanic eruptions in the highlands to the north and the expansionist dreams of our noisy neighbor, El Presidente Diaz of Mexico. But so far, and God willing, our two families seem to be coping well enough with the emergency.''

Captain Gringo waited until she'd served him before he took one polite sip, put the cup down, and said, "I'd better start at the beginning, then.''

He did, only leaving out the dirty parts as he brought Evita Barrios up-to-date on their misadventures. She was too polite to call him a liar, as Gaston confirmed his story with sage nods. But when she had it all she shook her head and insisted, "There must be some mistake. I know for a fact that the Barrios family is planning no trouble with the Cabreras.''

Captain Gringo shrugged and asked, "Can you speak for the Cabrera clan, Evita?''

She nodded soberly and said, "Sí. My maiden name was Cabrera. I am also a Barrios on my mother's side. My late husband and me were distant cousins. Does that shock you? It is not the custom for Creole aristocrats to marry beneath them, and there are only two aristocratic families in Guatemala, so . . .''

Captain Gringo shot a questioning look at Gaston, who shrugged and said, "Well, after people intermarry a bit they naturally tend to look more alike, non?''

"Was that an insult to my father's family, señor?'' asked Evita, with a more hurt than angry frown.

Gaston smiled gallantly and said, "Of course not, my adorable child! Everyone knows both the Barrios and Cabrera families are worthy of respect throughout Latin America!''

She sighed and said, "It is true I have distant cousins who may have a little Indio blood. The Cabreras are a very large group, and one must allow for a few black sheep in any family. But let us get back to this ridiculous idea that someone is expecting us to fight amongst ourselves. As you see, a feud between our families would be impossible as well as fatal to Guatemala! With all the troubles besetting our poor country, a strong central government is our only hope, and without our two intermarried families working together, there can be no government at all!''

Captain Gringo nodded but said, ''Try it this way, Evita. You just said the Cabreras have some less couth side branches out in the woods. Could those people who questioned us have had a plot within the much larger Cabrera clan? Black sheep sometimes *act* like black sheep, you know.''

Gaston brightened and said, ''Oui, it could get très fatigué to be a species of poor relation holding down a perhaps vital but low-ranking position, non? One of the things that makes running an army so interesting down here is that so many people want to be chief and nobody wants to be an Indian.''

Evita sighed and said, ''Well, we do have distant cousins indeed who call themselves Barrios or Cabrera. But no *important* member of either family could be plotting to . . . Just what *could* anyone be plotting, Dick?''

Captain Gringo shrugged and said, ''I don't know enough to even make an educated guess. Since you're in good with both families, why don't you just pass the warning on, for what it's worth, and let *them* figure it out? I know next to nothing about your country, and Gaston here seems a little out of touch since the last time he passed through.''

Evita nodded and said, ''Sí, I must send a message to the ruling junta, of course. Some of the older officers should remember Gaston, and once they know the story comes from a reliable source . . .''

She was sharp enough to catch the stricken look Gaston shot at the cooler Captain Gringo. So she asked, ''Did I suggest something wrong?''

Captain Gringo decided it was as good a time to bite the bullet as it would ever be. He smiled crookedly at her and said, "We'd just as soon the junta didn't hear about us, Evita. You see, Gaston and I haven't done anything against the interests of your country. But, well, your government didn't exactly give us permission to cross the border."

"You are *illegal immigrants,* to *Guatemala*?"

He laughed and said, "Just passing through. I assure you we're not after any banana picker's job. We were sent in from Mexico by a big international insurance company. We did the job they paid us to do. So now we just want to leave, sort of quietly."

She leaned back in her chair and said, "You'd better tell me about it," in a voice that sounded like she meant it. That was the trouble with Spanish beauties who were used to giving orders. They were used to giving orders.

Captain Gringo glanced at Gaston, who nodded, and told Evita, "Okay, you know Gaston here is a soldier of fortune. I'm one, too. We entered that volcanic disaster area up near the Mexican border to check things out for our employers, who had no interest in local politics. We would have gone back out the same way if we hadn't tangled with Mexican rurales and bandits."

She smiled thinly and said "That's a redundancy, Dick. Los rurales *are* bandits!"

He grinned and said, "Agreed. But we tangled with other bandits as well. As you probably know, the situation up there was an awful mess. So we had to help out some rescue workers from the International Red Cross when we found them having bandit trouble, too. We even helped some of your Guatemalan soldados fight off a nut called Caballero Blanco. We just didn't get around to telling them who we were, so I guess they thought we were Red Cross workers, too."

Her wide-set hazel eyes grew thoughtful and he wondered

what was going on right now in her lovely skull as she pressed him to go on. He said, "That's about it. We shot our way out and made it down here to meet an insurance rep and get paid off. We were just about to leave when those mysterious people jumped us and started talking about your family feud. Since we're not involved in it, there's no real reason to discuss us with the junta, right?"

"You must be Captain Gringo," she answered, wide-eyed with wonder.

He didn't answer.

She said, "We heard about your adventures up near the border, but nobody knew you were here in Guatemala City."

He sighed and said, "That was the general idea."

Gaston said, "I ask you, as an old comrade in arms of your late husband, to respect our, ah, continued existence, Señora Barrios."

She smiled radiantly and asked, "Are you both mad? Don't you know my poor country is fighting bandits, guerrillas, and foreign invasion, all at the same time? Of *course* I must tell my uncle, General Cabrera, that you are here! My brother-in-law, General Marin Lopez-Barrios, will be delighted, too!"

She sounded like she meant that, too. But a man had to try. So Captain Gringo said, "I sure wish you wouldn't, Evita. As I just said, we were planning on leaving quietly."

She shook her head and insisted, "Impossible. You were wrong about our soldados not knowing who it was who saved them up in the sierra. Nothing has been printed in the papers, of course. It only confuses the little people to read about such complicated matters, and, after all, when a Guatemalan officer is awarded a medal, he wishes all the credit as well. But just the other night our officers were talking about the way the two of you put Caballero Blanco out of business for our army, and I distinctly remember my uncle, the general, saying how much he admired you! Wait here. I must send one of my servants for to carry the good news to him!''

They rose as she did, of course. But when Captain Gringo headed for the door the moment she left the room, Gaston stopped him and asked, "What is wrong now? Didn't you hear her say her uncle wants to *hire* us?''

Captain Gringo growled, "She said no such thing. She only said he admired our style. I remember a rurale captain telling me the same thing, just before he ordered me shot!''

"True, but Guatemalans are more civilized, and it stands to reason that there is a market for our skills here, with the adorable egg about to hit the spinning fan, non?''

"The fan has too many blades,'' said Captain Gringo, taking out his pocket watch and glancing at it before putting it away again. He added, "It'll be dark soon. If anyone had followed us from the hotel, we'd have heard about it by now. I think a downhill run for the rail yards is our safest bet. We'll skip the depot and hop a freight for the lowlands, right?''

"Mais non! Don't be an idiot, Dick! If we cross the ruling junta double now, we shall have them as well as that mysterious gang after us!''

"How do we know the junta, or somebody in it, isn't behind said mysterious gang? This is getting complicated as a game of blind chess with an armed octopus, and we just *got* here! I vote we haul ass before that dame comes back. I hate long farewells.''

Gaston didn't get to vote one way or the other. Evita came back in, looking paler than they'd remembered, to say, "Something most strange is going on outside, Caballeros!''

The two soldiers of fortune exchanged throughtful looks as she explained, "My footman, Garcia, says he is afraid for to leave for my uncle's headquarters. He says this casa is being watched!''

"By who?'' asked Captain Gringo.

She said, "Quién sabe? Perhaps he is only imagining things. I saw no one when I looked out just now. But Garcia says there is someone in the casa across the calle.''

Gaston blinked in surprise and asked, "Is it unusual for someone to be home at this hour, Señora Evita?''

She nodded and said, "Sí. I know the family who owns that casa, of course. They have gone down to the coast for a family gathering. They have asked me and my servants for to keep an eye on their property while they are away. That is for why my footman, Garcia, knows there is someone over there. Garcia says he saw a lookout at an upstairs window just a while ago, before he informed the butler. Garcia says the man has a *rifle*! That is for why he is afraid to leave with a message.''

Captain Gringo nodded grimly and said, "Smart boy. What do you think, Gaston? Burglars? They could have heard the owners were away.''

Gaston pursed his lips thoughtfully and replied, "Burglars with rifles do not sound too professional, hein?''

Captain Gringo didn't think so either. But their hostess looked upset, so he soothed, "Take it easy, Evita. Whatever they are, they're in the house across the street, not *this* one. If they're just robbing the place, they should be leaving any minute.''

"But what if they do not leave, Dick? It is almost sunset, and once it gets dark . . .''

"Look, all your downstairs windows are well barred, right? Okay, Gaston and I are both armed. What about your household staff?''

"My late husband's hunting arms as well as his army

pistols are in his study, of course. But most of my servants are women. Only the footman and butler might know how to shoot a gun. I will call them.''

''Wait. Not yet. Never plan a gunfight when there's any other way out. You don't have a telephone, do you?''

''No, alas, this part of town has not been wired for them yet. We do not even have the new Edison lights up here on the ridge.''

''What about police patrols? How often do they come by, Evita?''

''When nobody *calls* for them, Dick? For why should la policía patrol this part of town? We are all most respectable up here.''

He grimaced and muttered, ''Oh boy. How do you feel about crawling over tile roofing, Gaston?''

Gaston shrugged and said, ''Eh bien, it is one of my favorite pastimes, assuming there is an adjoining house connected to this one.''

Captain Gringo shot the girl an inquiring look. She just looked up blankly at him. So he asked, ''Can you get to another house behind or beside this one without crossing open ground, Evita?''

She thought and said, ''There is an alley running behind this casa, of course. We are not crowded favilla dwellers, up here on the ridge, and one must have a breeze during the dry season. One might be able to leap from my roof to the one next door. It is perhaps two meters across the gap.''

Gaston looked sick. Captain Gringo said, ''Forget it. If they have the back alley staked out, a rooftop run could be injurious to one's health even if you *made* it!''

Evita leaned against Captain Gringo as she sobbed. ''Oh, what are we to do, Dick?''

He held her closer, since that felt better than anything else he could come up with at the moment, and said, "Nothing. If we can't get out, they can't get in. We don't have to worry about the patio, since none of us are about to be out there after dark. That leaves this thick-walled square fort. One guy with a gun in an upstairs room can cover anyone climbing one wall. Your two male servants, Gaston, and me add up to enough."

"Oh, no!" She sobbed. "There is no window at all on the south side of my casa. Only a chimney, covering most of the wall that way! What if they attack us from that side, Dick?"

He patted her trembling shoulder soothingly and asked, "With what? I remember the outside of this place now. I thought as we came across the street it looked solid as hell. They can't come through a window where there's no window. So we've got one armed man to spare for the only three directions they can hit us from."

"If you say so," she said with a shudder, adding, "Who do you think they are, Dick? And who could they be *after*?"

He started to say something dumb. But as soon as he considered how he and Gaston had stood with their backs to the mysterious house across the way, he had to reconsider. He said, "I don't know. They haven't told us yet. We'd better gather the household staff together for a council of war now."

She let go of him and went to gather her help as Gaston muttered, "Shame on you, Dick. You know who they are after as well as I do, non?"

Captain Gringo shook his head and said, "No, I don't. If they were in place over there before we showed up, how come we're still alive?"

"Merde alors! Don't upset a man with such remarks just before dinner, Dick! I assume, of course, we have time to eat like civilized people before we man the walls against the approaching species of whatever?"

"We'd better let the maid run sandwiches or something up to us. It figures to be getting dark pretty damned soon. Which approach do you figure we ought to have the best cover for, Gaston?"

"The rear, of course. There is no way in from the north or south. Hitting the front entrance calls for crossing the open patio after making the boom-boom getting in. On the other hand, the service entrance opens on the dark alley behind our glorious pink Alamo."

Captain Gringo nodded and said, "Right. We'll take turns guarding that approach. Butler and footman get to watch out for nuts who don't know what they're doing. We might be able to get the women to spell them once the moon's up. A dame doesn't have to know how to shoot a gun as long as she can scream good."

Gaston took out a smoke and lit up before he asked cautiously, "Have you considered the *other* way it works, Dick?"

"You mean the other side really being after Evita Barrios? Sure. Pantera said enough for us to guess a family feud's about to start, no matter what the family heads think. So what?"

"So what if you and I simply strolled out the front, arm in arm? I have reconsidered what you said before about getting ourselves out of this pickle before the shooting starts, Dick. It is still daylight outside. As you observed, they would have behaved more rudely if it had been *us* they were really after, hein?"

Captain Gringo shook his head and said, "Forget it. In the

first place, it would be a shitty way to treat a lady who just served us tea. In the second, they *could* be after us. You want to find out the hard way?''

"Well, not if you put it that way."

Staring down into a pitch-black alley soon got boring as hell. But it had to be done, and Captain Gringo had lost, when Gaston had flipped him for first watch at the upstairs rear window.

The guys at the other two windows had it better. They'd lit the patio lamps at sunset to give the old butler, covering the front, a pretty good field of fire in case anyone was dumb enough to come over the front wall from the well-lit avenue. The footman, covering the slit between the houses to the north, had a shaft of light from a streetlamp and one of the late colonel's shotguns to work with. So if anyone was planning a call on the widow without a card to present at the front entrance, they should be hitting the rear service entrance almost anytime now. A big orange tropic moon was rising above the rooftops to the east and the alley didn't figure to stay pitch black forever.

Captain Gringo had opted for a twelve-gauge pump gun loaded with number-nine buck, in addition to his double-action .38, of course. He knew the service entrance was solid oak to begin with and barricaded on the inside with kitchen furniture piled against a heavy butcher's block. So even if he couldn't see so hot, it was hard to see how anyone was about to bust in the back without catching a mess of the late colonel's hunting ammo.

He heard something move down there and held his breath to listen better. The trick of spotting something in the dark, he knew, was not to look directly in the direction of a sound but sort of off to one side. The corners of the human eye were more sensitive to movement if there was light enough to see anything at all.

There wasn't. It was so damned black down there that he was starting to see pale floaters inside his dilated eyes. A sort of ghostly purple fuzz ball drifted slowly across the alley as he strained his ears so hard he could hear his own pulse inside his head. He had to take a breath. It sounded like a locomotive bleeding steam. But the sound he'd heard down there didn't repeat itself as he held his breath some more. He decided it had to be an alley cat, a rat, or something. If he'd heard a human being, the bastard for sure wasn't busting down any doors.

As keyed up as he was, he nearly jumped out of his skin when the door behind him opened and Gaston said, "Eh bien, neither the cook nor any of the serving maids seems to admire me, and I am tired of dozing on the couch downstairs. I'll take over now."

Captain Gringo rose from the window seat, stiff from holding such a cramped position for the past few hours. He said, "Be my guest. There's either a very noisy cat or a very quiet guy pussyfooting around down there. But the moonlight's about to improve the situation in an hour or so. The shotgun on the sill is on safe, but there's a round in the chamber."

Gaston groped his way into position as his eyes adjusted to the darkness of the blacked-out guest room. He stared out and muttered, "Merde alors, there could be an *army* down there and one could not prove it by me!"

Captain Gringo nodded and said, "It's a pretty uninspiring view. But look on the bright side. I don't think they're coming. Not this early, at any rate. We're smack in town and Latins are night people. They won't risk any serious moves until after midnight, when the neighbors start turning into pumpkins.''

Gaston objected, ''If they wait that long, the moon will be beaming directly down at the rear entrance, non?''

'''For a while. By three or four in the morning it'll be over on the other side of the sky and dark as hell down there again.''

Gaston grimaced and said, ''I wish you would not say things like that, Dick. But my dear old aunt Mimi, the one who introduced me to oral sex and knife fighting, often said the best time to break and enter was four in the morning, when the innocents among us are most apt to be sleeping as soundly as they ever manage.''

Captain Gringo moved to the hall door as he said, ''Yeah; I'll kip out for a couple of hours and relieve you before then. Have you checked the other posts up here?''

''Oui, one of the chambermaids is already manning the old butler's position up front. The footman has arranged something with the cook for later. One hopes that means she will take his place at the window for a time. She's too old and fat for him to be interested in any other way.''

Captain Gringo cracked the door, intending to slip out quickly to avoid outlining Gaston at the window with the hall light any longer than he had to. But when Gaston started to say something else he shut the door again, muttering, ''Jesus, don't you ever stop talking?''

Gaston chuckled and replied, ''Only while I am masturbating. What I was about to suggest is that we put an end to this farce so we can all get some sleep, hein?''

Captain Gringo frowned and said, ''If you're suggesting Muhammad going to the mountain, forget it. Let the cocksuckers come to us! That house they're holed up in is just as solid a fort as this one.''

Gaston said, "Oui, but they don't *own* it. So, should the local police arrive in numbers, tweeting whistles and so forth, one may assume they would fade into the favilla on the far side of the ridge long before any officer of the law could question their unauthorized occupation of the premises, non?"

"How do you call a cop without a telephone in Guatemala City?"

"With this adorable shotgun, of course. A volley of twelve-gauge would surely arouse the undivided attention of any police official within a mile or more, non?"

Captain Gringo shook his head and said, "I thought of that hours ago. Forget it. Three reasons. The cops would no doubt be interested as hell. But it could take them a hell of a while to pinpoint where the shots were coming from and then decide to do anything about them. Meanwhile, the guys after us or the widow would have no reason to pussyfoot, and might hit us harder and faster than I like to think about. The third reason, of course, is that I'm not sure we *want* to explain shots in the night, or *ourselves,* to any local cops, either!"

Gaston sighed and said, "Eh bien, you are right. I talk too much." So Captain Gringo slipped out of the room before he could think of something else to say.

The big Yank hadn't taken time to explore the whole house. But he knew the big leather couch in the main drawing room was long enough for him to stretch out on, and he'd promised to relieve Gaston in a few hours. So he headed for the stairwell. But before he reached it a side door opened and Evita Barrios stepped partway out to ask if she could see him a minute. He could surely see *her* a minute. She was wearing a thin black-lace kimono, and the lamplight from the room behind her was shining through it teasingly. He'd *thought* she had to have a great pair of legs. But they were even shapelier than he'd imagined. And Captain Gringo had a good imagination.

He followed her into her bedroom and didn't comment when she shut and barred the door behind him. He knew the rules down here and she was breaking one of them already. Nicely brought up Spanish girls didn't visit alone with men they weren't related to, even fully dressed, behind an unlocked door. But this wasn't exactly a social situation. So he decided he'd better keep his hands to himself until he found out just what she had in mind.

She invited him to sit down. The only seat, aside from her four-poster bed, was a bitty stool by her dressing table that looked too sissy to hold a man his size. So he sat on the bed. She looked a bit startled and remained on her feet, saying, "I am afraid I have nothing refreshing for to offer you, up here, Dick."

He smiled up at her and said, "I'll be the judge of that. What can I do for *you*, Evita?"

She said, "I have been thinking about what you said about some sort of family feud. Since I was married to a Barrios, no Cabrera who was plotting anything would see fit to let me in on it, no?"

"You're learning. I think it was Machiavelli who said two people could keep a secret if one of them was dead."

She repressed a shudder and sat down beside him as she asked in a worried tone, "Do you think someone thinks I know something my Barrios in-laws should not know?"

"Someone's either after you or after Gaston and me. *We* don't know beans. So what do *you* know, Evita?"

She really shuddered, this time. So he put an arm around her shoulders to comfort her as she sobbed. "Nothing! I did not even know, before you told me, that there was supposed to *be* any trouble between my two families!"

He held her a little closer, inhaling some of the musky perfume she'd apparently put on for some reason just before bedtime, and suggested she think a little harder, adding, "Look, relative or not, you were married to a big-shot Barrios for . . . how long, Evita?"

"About three years. My late husband, while very sweet, was a bit older than me. The woman he was married to when he and Gaston fought together under Presidente Justo Barrios died of the vomito negro while I was still in my teens. He married me. Then *he* died of the vomito negro, too. Have you ever had the fever, Dick?"

He nodded and said, "Yeah; we call it yellow jack. I got it not long after I came down here from the States. I guess everybody does, sooner or later."

She snuggled closer and said, "I know. I had it when I was just a little girl, and it almost killed me. But since then, of course, I have been immune."

He nodded and said, "Yeah, the only nice thing anyone can say about yellow jack is that you can't catch it twice."

Then he frowned thoughtfully and said, "Hold it. Didn't you just say your late husband was much older than you, Evita?"

"Sí, he was old enough for to be my father, but it was a good marriage anyway. He was a handsome and muy toro man in the prime of life and . . ."

"And he died of yellow jack in late middle age?" Captain Gringo cut in, adding, "How old was his first wife when she died of the same thing, Evita?"

She shrugged and said, "I don't know. Forty or so, I suppose. Why?"

He said, "It doesn't work. I can see *one* native-born Central American making it to middle age before catching endemic yellow jack. Two makes it one too many. Most of you people are immune to your homegrown fevers by the time they're ten or twelve, right?''

She frowned thoughtfully and said, "I caught vomito negro when I was eight or nine. But some of my friends and relations have never had it at all, Dick."

He nodded but insisted, "Sure. But anyone who's never had yellow jack down here was simply *born* immune to it. I've seen very few North Americans or Europeans get through a rainy season down here without coming down with yellow jack. Most pick it up within a year and either die or get better and never have it again. You natives all have it when you're still kids, if you ever have it at all. So tell me how your Guatemalan husband and his Guatemalan first wife both died of the same fever in middle age, and we can *forget* bismuth in their hot chocolate!''

"Bizz-what in hot chocolate, Dick?"

"Bismuth poisoning makes you puke black while it's killing you. It doesn't turn your skin yellow and you don't run much of a fever, but to the average doctor down here I guess vomito negro must be a more common complaint than bismuth poisoning, right?''

She gasped. "Oh, my God! Are you suggesting someone poisoned my husband, Dick?''

"You were there. What do you think? He was a big shot in the Barrios clan, right?''

"Sí, a member of the junta! But he died almost a year ago, and his first wife even earlier! You say this mysterious feud hasn't really started yet, no?''

"Maybe my information wasn't exactly up-to-date. Someone must have been plotting something for some time for the news to have gotten out. That dame who asked which side I was on couldn't have been on either, or she'd have had no reason to question me. The people who sent her must be a party of the third part, aiming to cash in on the mess. So let's talk about that, Evita. Who'd be most likely to take over the country if the current clique wiped itself out in a War of the Roses?''

She said, ''Nobody! Between them the Barrios and Cabrera factions have every important government and military position how you say sewed up! If my relations on both sides were to go to war with one another, the result would be total chaos and, oh, Dick, I am so *frightened*!''

She must have been. She started to cry. So he held her closer to comfort her, and somehow, the next thing they knew, they were flat on the mattress together and he was kissing her warmly.

She kissed back, with considerable enthusiasm, and didn't seem to mind when he slipped a free hand inside her kimono top to comfort a bare firm breast as well. But when he slid it down her smooth warm flesh to work on the knot holding her dumb kimono together in front, she stiffened, rolled her face to one side, and asked him what he was doing. It was too dumb a question to answer, and he noticed she made no move to stop him as he unfastened her sash and let her black lace fall out of the way. But as he ran his palm down across her soft bare belly to cup her warm fuzzy mons, she tried to cross her creamy thighs and protested, ''No! Wait! I am still in mourning, Querido!''

He said, ''That's all right. I'm not asking you to marry me,'' as he parted her thatch with two fingers to gently rock the man in the boat.

Her clit was already engorged. So he knew she was sort of fibbing when she protested, ''Stop it! I wasn't expecting anything like this at all! Are you trying to take advantage of a poor helpless widow, you brute?''

He said, ''Yeah,'' and kissed her again as she went through

the socially approved motions of gently trying to push him away with her hands while she spread her thighs and thrust her pelvis up to enjoy the petting. He tongued her experimentally, and when she tried to suck his tongue out by the roots, he assumed it was safe to make a grab for his own belt. Naturally, by the time he had his pants down enough to matter, Evita had her damned fool legs crossed again and they had to start all over. But Gaston wasn't expecting him for a couple of hours, and it only took three or four minutes to get her thighs apart again.

But as he started to mount her, Evita protested, "Not with your jacket and shoulder holster on, for God's sake!" So he laughed and let go of her to sit up and shuck himself right. She took advantage of the lull in the action to roll over on her belly and bury her blushing face in the pillows. Some dames were like that, with the lights on.

He considered getting up to trim the bedroom lamp. But the lamp was across the room and Evita's lace-covered derriere was here and now. So he rolled into position above it, lifted the lace out of the way, and parted her soft buttocks with his palms to make room for his questing shaft. As it felt its way in, Evita gasped and protested, "No! Not that way!" Then, as she felt where it was going, she arched her spine to take it doggy with a girlish giggle, adding, "Oh, I thought you wanted to abuse me in the Greek fashion. This is still most improper, but . . . Madre de Dios, is all that really meant for poor little me?"

He grinned down at her lace-covered back and bare buttocks as he moved in and out of her faster. Thanks to the awful things that dame at the hotel had done to it earlier, he was hard as a brick and she felt tighter than she probably would have normally. But, despite her complimentary remarks about his size, it didn't seem to faze her. She started beating the mattress with her clenched fists as she whimpered, "Oh, you terrible man! You should not be doing this to a respectable widow in mourning, but, could you get it in a little deeper?"

He gripped her hips and moved them back until his feet were on the rug and he had her up on her knees with her elevated derriere in position for some real old-fashioned acrobatics. She gasped in mingled wonder and delight and shoved back to meet his pounding while she insisted that he was a shameless brute with no respect for highborn ladies. There was no way a man in his position could defend himself from such a charge. So he just kept quiet and pounded her to glory. He came first. It was easy and just as well. When Evita climaxed, she fell off his still-unsated erection to lie moaning, face down, about the way he'd abused her hospitality.

He wanted to abuse it some more. So he got on the bed again with her and rolled her over on her back. She protested, "Oh, not with the light on! I feel so naked, Dick!"

She *looked* pretty naked, too, now that the dumb kimono was out of the way, save for her upper arms. He grinned down at her lush ivory charms and remounted her, soothing, "Relax, you've still got your kimono on, sort of."

She laughed, despite herself, and started to struggle out of it. He wasn't laying anybody with his hands. So he helped, and when she was free to wrap her bared arms as well as her legs around him, she sighed and said, "Sí, it does feel ever so much nicer without that scratchy lace in the way. But I'll have you know I don't do this with *every* man I pour tea for, you mean old thing!"

He nuzzled her neck and moved faster in her as he replied, "I should hope not. But you sure move nice for a lady who hasn't been getting any lately."

"Don't be beastly, you beast. I'll have you know you are the first man to have me since my husband died, and I assure you I was a virgin when I married him!"

He kissed her some more to shut her up. He didn't care about her past sex life. What she was doing with her internal contractions here and now was more important. He groped blindly for a pillow and shoved it under her hips to enjoy her to the full as he felt himself getting there again. She pleaded, "Not *that* deep, dammit! You are hitting bottom with every stroke and . . . Oh, Jesus, Maria, y José! Forget what I just said and do it, do it, do it, *dooooo* it!"

Captain Gringo's legs felt sort of rubbery, and he hadn't gotten nearly as much rest as he'd planned, but his pecker, at least, felt a lot better when he relieved Gaston at the rear window a few hours later.

Gaston growled, "Sacrebleu, it's about time you came!"

Captain Gringo laughed and said, "I couldn't come again right now on a bet. What's going on outside?"

"Merde alors, if anything had been going on you would have heard me shooting at it, non? Regard the moonlight illuminating the alley très romantique. I think I heard some alley cats making love a while ago. No doubt the full moon inspired them. So far, it has failed to inspire our mysterious friends across the way, if they are still across the way. Has it occurred to you yet that this whole affair could be but the hunting of the snipe?"

"More than once, when it was my turn at that fucking window. That's the trouble with guard duty. Nine times out of ten you're guarding against nothing. But that tenth time can *gitcha*! Move your ass and let me take over for a while."

Gaston stood up, stretched, and said, "I am hungry and I have a most astounding erection for a man my age. I wonder if that fat cook would see fit to at least feed me."

The little Frenchman sniffed, frowned, and added, "That's odd. I seem to smell something naughty. Didn't you wash yourself after that mystery woman at the hotel, Dick?"

"Well, I just had time for a whore bath, and it's a pretty warm night."

"You can say that again. Are you holding out on your dear old mentor about one of the maids, my bashful youth?"

Captain Gringo chuckled and said, "I give you my word I haven't been messing with any of the servants."

Then he took his place at the window, turning his grinning face away from Gaston, who shrugged and said, "Eh bien, perhaps I'll have better luck. The girls should be manning the other posts now, non?"

"God damn it, Gaston, you know better than to mess with a guard on post, don't you?"

"Spoilsport. Very well, the fat cook may not look as ugly in the dark, and, after all, they say the way to a man's heart is through his stomach, hein?"

Captain Gringo resisted the impulse to tell Gaston to behave himself. For one thing, it would have hardly been fair, now, and for another, Gaston never listened to him about pussy anyway.

But it was something else to worry about after Gaston left him alone and he got tired of staring down into an alley that didn't look much more interesting even by moonlight.

Now that he'd had time to cool down after his roll in the feathers with Evita, he remembered all too well how seriously Latin men took such matters. He doubted like hell that Evita was likely to play true confessions. But if old Gaston banged one of the serving wenches, or, worse yet, tried and failed, there was no telling who might hear about it. What they'd *do* about it, if the babbling dame was a blood relative, was less of a mystery.

But Gaston, despite his flippant way of killing time with his mouth, was an older tropic hand than Captain Gringo and had gotten in trouble over many a Latin temptress before his younger comrade in arms had been born. So when he left the big Yank and made a professional tour of the other posts, he was strictly business.

The maid in the front room offered no temptation in any case, since the old butler was kipped out on a cot in the corner while the worried little mestiza sat at the window with a shotgun too big for her across her lap. Gaston moved over to stare past her down into the patio and told her to keep up the good work. She said, "Oh, Señor, I am so afraid."

Gaston placed a fatherly hand on her trembling shoulder and said, "All good soldados are afraid, Muchacha. But regard, there is no way for them to get at you without a scaling ladder, hein?"

"What if they *bring* a scaling ladder, Señor?"

"I suggest you scream, très loudly. But do not concern your pretty head with such grotesque notions, little one. With all due respect, we posted you here because we don't expect anyone to try and cross the illuminated patio. Let the old man sleep a little longer. Then wake him up and tell him to take your place."

He left and moved down the hall to the end room. Another maid was at the end window, alone. He asked her where the footman was. She said she had no idea. She seemed calm as well as disturbingly pretty. So Gaston didn't see fit to pat her in a fatherly or any other way. He just told her to keep up the good work and went downstairs to the kitchen.

There was nobody there. No problem for an old trail cook.

Gaston lit a lamp, saw that the beehive oven and/or cooking hearth was cold, and philosophically proceeded to build himself a tortilla-and-cold-beef sandwich.

He was washing it down with cold but strong black coffee when a voice behind him demanded to know what he was doing in her kitchen. He turned and managed not to laugh as he saw the fat mestiza cook standing there in a thin night-gown and her big brown bare feet.

Gaston waved the half-eaten sandwich and said, "I did not wish to disturb you, Querida. But, as you see, a man has to eat."

She tried not to smile as she said, "I am not your querida. I have no hombre these days. You should not be in my kitchen without my permiso, Señor. You should have awakened me if you wished for something to eat. My room is just next door, eh?"

Gaston smiled gallantly and said, "Mais non! It would never do for a caballero to come calling on a señorita in her own bedchamber at this hour! What would the neighbors think? One must be most discreet about such matters, and, alas, you have never given me any hint encouraging my advances!"

The cook laughed girlishly and said, "Idioto, do I look like the kind of woman who has to worry about men sneaking into her bedchamber?"

Gaston said, "I don't know. Twirl around and let me have a better look at you, Querida."

She did no such thing. She heaved a fat sigh and said, "Do not mock a poor old woman, Señor. There was a time, I know you will find this hard to believe, when I *did* have to beat the men off. Alas, I fear I did too good a job. When a girl is young and beautiful she thinks she has all the time in the world for to wait for the right man to come along. But the years of our lives slip so swiftly through our fingers and . . ."

"I am older than you, Querida," Gaston said gently, putting his food and drink aside as he moved closer. "I used to be young and beautiful too. Then one day I looked in the mirror to see a dirty old man staring back at me. But dirty old men need love and affection too."

"Stop!" She gasped as he took her in his arms, with some effort because of the way she filled them with her elephantine girth. She protested, "We are all alone down here, and I am still a virgin!"

"Mon Dieu, what a terrible thing for a pretty little thing like you to live with!" said Gaston, even as he realized he'd never in this world be able to even kiss her unless she moved her head forward across those massive breasts toward him.

She said, "Let me go! Help yourself to anything you want in here. But let me go back to bed, you maniac!"

She started to leave. There was no way a man Gaston's size was about to stop her without hurting them both. So he simply held on and let her half-carry him with her as she charged out of the kitchen and into her bedroom. There was no lamp lit inside. So Gaston kicked the door shut after them with a heel, in passing, and her momentum carried them across the little chamber in the darkness until their knees hit the edge of the bed and they both crashed down on it.

By some miracle, the springs held, although they still bounced awesomely for a while as he groped and she struggled. Then suddenly she went limp with a vast whale-spout sigh as the Frenchman got one small bony hand between her big fat thighs and proceeded to explore her inner being with skilled fingers.

She lay back, her huge rump presenting her wide-open entrance to the ceiling as Gaston got on his knees between hers, took a deep breath, and dove head first to see what a fat forty-five-year-old virgin might taste like.

She hissed, "Oh, my God, that's a crime against nature!" as he assured himself that, although clean, she didn't really mean what she'd said about being a virgin. He started peeling off his own clothes as he kept her in position, moaning in ecstasy, the way his dear old aunt Mimi had when everyone in the world was younger. He brought her to orgasm in his polite French way, then slid up her mountainous body, peeling off her gown on the way, to settle atop her at what might have been an alarming distance from the mattress had the lamp been lit.

As he entered her, the fat cook sobbed. "Oh, God, I can't believe it, after all this time! Are you really inside me, Querido?"

"I am doing my best to *get* there, ma chérie. Could you, ah, spread your thighs a little wider?"

She could. But Gaston could only get two-thirds of it in, because of all the lard in the way. Fortunately, Gaston was well hung despite his stature, so his so-called virgin was enjoying more shaft than she might have in the recent past, and it was driving her wild. It was doing awesome things to the bedsprings, too. So, once they'd come old-fashioned, she saw the common sense of doing it right, on the floor, dog-style. Since that offered a much better angle of attack, Gaston was able to satisfy himself as well in that position, and she said she'd never known before that a man could get it in that deep. Gaston resisted a laconic remark about that being a reasonable assumption on the part of a virgin. It was not true all cats were gray in the dark. But from this angle one could pretend one was rutting with a human being instead of a walrus, and she felt human indeed, where it counted.

Having satisfied himself, and now thoroughly ashamed of

himself, Gaston was only being polite when the fat cook dragged him back up on the bed to cuddle. She felt like at least three women in bed with him. But when he absently reached for a breast to fondle, he only found two, each the size of a beach ball. She wanted to fondle him, too, and he had to admit she gave a great hand job, for a virgin. So maybe he wasn't so ashamed of himself after all.

But he wasn't ready for another mating with a walrus just yet. So he said, "Let us just rest in one another's arms for a time, my adorable little cabbage. I forgot to make sure the door was locked."

"We are alone on this floor," she assured him, adding, "All the other servants and la señora are upstairs, no?"

Gaston said, "All but the footman. He was not at his post just now. Where is his room, my pet?"

She said, "Oh, he is not here. He went out some time ago."

"He *what*?" Gaston frowned, adding, "When did all this happen, and why were we not informed?"

She snuggled closer and replied innocently, "I thought you knew. He said as much when I heard him in the kitchen and asked where he was going."

Gaston sat bolt upright, groped on his pants, grabbed for his .38 in the dark, and ran outside, barefoot and shirtless, as his fat paramour called something after him he didn't have time to listen to. He got to the service entrance and, yes, the barricade had been shoved aside. The back door, while still stout, wasn't even *barred* now!

He tested the latch. The door was unlocked. He swore, locked it, and ran back to the cook's room to finish dressing. She asked him what was wrong and he told her to get dressed, too, poco tiempo. Then he ran out and took the stairs two at a time. As he dashed in to join Captain Gringo he blurted, "We have been crossed double! That species of a footman who told us about mysterious strangers across the street has just run off to meet someone in the darkness before dawn! Worse yet, he may have left some time ago!"

Captain Gringo glanced down into the alley, saw that it was still deserted, and got to his feet, saying, "Right. I *thought* I heard someone pussyfooting around down there while it was still dark. Who told you all this, Gaston?"

"The cook. She's not in on it. She's merely a sex maniac who should be on a diet. I don't see how anyone else in the house at the moment could be in on it either. But the son of a poxed camel left the back door unlocked. Do you want a diagram on a blackboard, Dick?"

Captain Gringo shook his head and said, "Haven't time for the fine print. It'll be dark back there in less than an hour. You round up the servants and get 'em down to the patio. I'll rouse Evita and get her dressed!"

They split up in the hallway. Captain Gringo charged into Evita's bedroom to find her, of course, naked and sleeping. He lit the lamp after slamming the door and shook her awake, saying, "Rise and shine, Sleeping Beauty. Got to get out of the castle before the wicked witch shows up with a dragon, or worse!"

"What on earth are you talking about, Dick? Let me wake up a bit if you wish for to make love to me again."

He shook her harder and snapped, "Later, after we see if we're still *alive*! Your footman's whole story was a ruse. Get your damned duds on and I'll tell you about it on the way! Come on, doll, move!"

She did. So he had her at least half-dressed when he hauled her down to the front entrance, where Gaston and the others were waiting. The old butler had a big box he said was full of the family jewels. Captain Gringo said, "Good thinking. Do you have much cash in the place, Evita?"

She shook her head and said, "No; I keep my money in the bank and pay by check, of course. But won't you tell me what this is all about, Dick?"

"Later. Gaston, you want to take the point?"

"Oui. Since great minds run from the same bogies, I assume our best bet would be the last place we would be going if we believed that lying footman."

"Don't lecture me on *tactics*, dammit, *move*!"

So Gaston moved. He crossed the avenue at an innocent walk, one of the late colonel's hunting rifles down at his side like an umbrella, and, when nobody shot at him, made quick work of the front lock of the deserted house across the way. As he stepped inside, Captain Gringo warned the others not to move out until Gaston signaled that the other house was really clear. Evita protested, "We can't go over *there*! That is where Garcia said the gang was hiding!"

"That's how I know they're not, I hope," said Captain Gringo, going on to explain, "Your footman knew the place was empty. He made up the story about spotting someone with a rifle over there because he wanted us to do just what we did. So now that we've done it, it's time to do something else!"

Gaston lit a match across the street. Captain Gringo said, "Bueno. He'd signal some other way if someone was forcing him to. Let's go, gang. Stay close together and just walk over like we've been invited to a party, see?"

"At three-thirty in the morning, Dick?" asked Evita. But he just shoved her out ahead of him and within minutes they were gathered with Gaston in the patio across the way.

Gaston said, "I just checked the back. Solid stucco. No

doubt the people who live here do not enjoy visits from the slums down the other side of the slope, hein?''

Captain Gringo nodded and said, ''They probably *did* check the place out, and gave up on it when they saw the only way in or out was exposed to the lit-up avenue. Okay, the moon won't be going down again for at least forty-five minutes and it looks like we made it unobserved. Let's find us some windows overlooking the other house, and we shall see what we shall see.''

They went into the main house and barricaded the doors. The barred first-story windows called for fewer precautions. Captain Gringo told everyone to follow him as he led the way upstairs. He found the master bedroom locked, and neither he nor Gaston could pick it. So he kicked it open. As he crossed the deserted bedroom to the jalousied windows, Evita followed, saying it made her feel like a thief to be in her neighbors' home without their permiso. He opened one slat of the jalousies and saw he had a nice field of fire covering both this place's patio and Evita's house across the way. He told her, ''You say they're friends of yours. So they'll understand, Evita.''

She said, ''I wish *I* did, Dick! Why did we have to rush out of my house in such a hurry at this hour?''

He said, ''Because in about forty-five minutes, or less, the other side will make their move. Your treacherous footman not only left the back door open, he can tell his pals who's at what window with what, see?''

Like Gaston, who'd taken a position at the window on the far side of the empty bed, Captain Gringo had exchanged the short-range twelve-gauge for a .30-30 hunting rifle before leaving the Barrios house across the way. As he experimentally eased the muzzle between the jalousie slats, Evita gasped and said, "Be careful! Don't break my neighbor's blinds, Dick! Can't you just *open* them?"

He shook his head and said, "Your treacherous footman knows damned well your neighbors closed them before they left. They were closed when he made up that story about spotting a guy with a gun up here in this room."

She insisted, "But you say they mean to attack my house from the back alley, no?"

He said, "Honey, I don't know *what* the hell they mean to do! Very few guerrillas go to West Point. I learned while fighting Apache to just cover all bets and hope the other side hasn't got a fifth ace up its sleeve."

Gaston, at the other window, simply shoved the muzzle of his own rifle through the jalousies, breaking two slats, as he observed, "I smell something rotten in Denmark as well as a fifth ace, Dick. As I regard that other house from this distance, my nose tells me we must be missing something. They can't just be planning an old-fashioned rush."

"Not unless they're maniacs," Captain Gringo agreed, adding, "I know *I'd* hesitate to rush a pile of masonry like that, even if it was out in open country. How long do you figure a firefight is good for in this fashionable part of town?"

Gaston shrugged and replied, "Before the police arrive in droves? Five minutes would be taking a chance. Perhaps they merely plan a volley from the alley into the rear window they think you or me will be manning?"

"That's a lot of trouble and a hell of a chance to take for a fifty-fifty crack at only one of us, Gaston. We locked the service entrance again before we pulled out. So there goes any fun and games with a firebomb. That couldn't be the plan anyway. Anyone with a lick of sense could see we might notice the barricade had been removed before the footman could lead them back from wherever.''

Gaston shrugged and said, ''We are talking in the circle. I just *said* that other house was one tough nut to crack, non?''

''It would be if we were still holed up in it, and let's hope they think we are. Maybe they're just jerk-offs some smarter sneak has duped into a suicide attack?''

Evita asked, ''What would be the point, Dick?''

So he said, ''Causing trouble. Even if they didn't get you or any of your innocent help, your relatives on both sides would certainly get excited about someone even *trying* to smoke up the widow of a junta officer, see?''

She didn't, but Gaston nodded and said, ''Oui, even a bungled assassination attempt calls for the usual mass arrests and sudden drumhead court-martials. That's the smartest suggestion I've heard so far, Dick. La Señora is related to both factions. What time is it? How are we doing with that moon?''

Captain Gringo said, ''The alley behind Evita's place should be almost dark enough by now. Let's hope they'll settle for some busted glass and pockmarked pink stucco. Let's hope they haven't picked *this* direction as a getaway route, too!''

Before Gaston could reply, they all heard the clip-clop of steel-shod hooves on pavement. Captain Gringo eased another slat open for a better look as he muttered, ''What the hell? Isn't it a little early for the milk wagon?''

Evita said, ''It sounds like a carriage horse. Someone must be coming home from downtown rather late, no?''

Gaston, closer to the sounds, said, ''I see it. Horse-drawn two-wheel cart of some kind, covered with a tarpaulin. Four men riding it. Dressed peon. Farmers bringing produce into town?''

Captain Gringo asked Evita if there was a market of any kind to the north. She said there wasn't. He shrugged and said, "Okay, maybe they delivered something closer to the center of town and now they're headed home. But cover them anyway, Gaston."

"Merde alors, teach your grandmother how to knit!"

The mysterious horse-drawn vehicle moved innocently up the avenue until it was right out front. Then it stopped, and Captain Gringo said, "Oh boy! Hold your fire, Gaston. They're getting down. They're not looking this way. They may just want to grease an axle or something."

"Do you believe that, Dick?"

"No, but let 'em make the first hostile move."

They did. As one of the cotton-clad men unhitched the horse, the others swung the apparent wagon tongue around and dropped it to the pavement. Captain Gringo gasped and said, "Jeeeezusss!" as they whipped the tarp off to reveal a four-pounder field gun, aimed right at the Barrios house across the street!

Both soldiers of fortune opened fire with their rifles at once, of course. Captain Gringo's second round hit the gunner holding the lanyard in his side. But as the son of a bitch went down he pulled the lanyard, and the field gun went off with an ear-splitting roar!

It was impossible to miss Evita's house at point-blank. So her windows across the street lit up like jack-o'-lantern eyes as the shell exploding inside blew her roof skyward in a cloud of shattered tiles.

Then it got very quiet for a time as the dust settled and the survivors gazed soberly down at the four still forms on the pavement around the still-smoking silent field gun. But the silence didn't last long. Dogs started barking, doors and windows started flying open, and people all around started yelling. Captain Gringo hauled the late colonel's rifle back inside and lit a claro as Gaston said, "Eh bien, if *that* didn't wake up the local police and at least a company of soldados, nothing ever will! Do we run for it or stay and hope they'll accept us as friends of the family, Dick?"

It was a good question. Captain Gringo looked thoughtfully at Evita and said, "There's no place to run to. Every man in town with hair on his chest and a gun in his hand will be headed this way from every direction by now. I guess we'll just have to hope Evita here still has a little political clout in Guatemala City."

She did. As Captain Gringo had predicted, uniformed men with guns came charging in from every compass point, and things got a little tense until Evita explained the situation to her cousins on both sides of her family tree. But once they got the picture, officers named both Barrios and Cabrera kept slapping Captain Gringo and Gaston on the back and telling them what swell guys they were.

By sunrise Evita and her servants had been taken under the wing of other relations down the avenue and the two soldiers of fortune had been escorted to military headquarters downtown, a wistful distance from the railroad depot. It seemed a four-star general wanted to see them. Nobody saw fit to disarm them, and the officer of the day told them they had the run of the post. But they didn't think that included *leaving*, via the closely guarded gates.

Four-star generals didn't get to the office early. So they had time to eat breakfast and hang around the dayroom a few hours. They were both used to going as long as seventy-two hours without sleep if anything at all interesting was going

on. But waiting for his nibs to shower, shit, and shave got
tedious as hell toward the end. The only interesting item in
the officers' dayroom was an early edition of the oddly named
local paper, *La Prenza*, meaning "The Truth." What *La
Prenza* had printed about the incident at the hotel was either a
cover-up or mighty sloppy police procedure. The paper said
that an unidentified mestizo had been found in an alley and
didn't mention the hotel at all. If the cops had picked up
Pantera, they were keeping it to themselves. But the paper did
say that witnesses had identified the killer as a woman, and
theorized that the whole thing had been a crime of passion.
Captain Gringo thought the dame had come to and gotten
away before the cops arrived. Gaston protested in an injured
tone that he was sure he'd kicked her harder than *that*!

There was no mention of the guys Gaston had left in other
alleyways in other parts of town. That worked more than one
way. The local law could be sitting on the story, or, just as
likely, others in the mystery gang might have gotten there
first. Pantera had intimated that she worked for a serious
outfit.

A junior officer came in to tell them the general would see
them now. So they followed him across the parade to GHQ.

On the way there, Gaston mused softly, in English, "The
people at the hotel might have shoved our old friend Paco out
a window to preserve their good name, non?"

Captain Gringo muttered, "Utshay upshay. Sometimes when
you don't talk about a headache it goes away all by itself,
right?"

The aide ushered them into a cavernous room that came
with a wall map and a mahogany desk almost as big. A
gray-haired fat man wearing a uniform fancy enough for a
New York doorman was seated behind it as they entered, but
rose to greet them with handshakes and a friendly smile. The

junior officer vanished discreetly. So they knew the big cheese wanted a private conversation with them.

The general offered them Havana perfectos and comfortable seats across the desk from his own swivel chair. He waited until they'd all lit up and settled back before he said, ''I have been going over your dossiers, Señores, and I must say I am most impressed. Is it true you once wrecked the entire Mexican railroad system?''

Captain Gringo smiled modestly and replied, ''Not every mile of it, Sir, and they started the fight.''

The Guatemalan general chuckled and said, ''El Presidente Diaz makes a habit of starting fights with people, it would seem. Since you just came down from our devastated northwest provinces, you naturally know the situation up there. Our agents report our neighbors to the north are planning to take advantage of the earthquake and volcanic disaster. Mexican engineers at this moment are pushing a narrow-gauge railroad through the Sierra Madres, they say, to assure relief supplies into the stricken area.''

Captain Gringo frowned and asked, ''Why, General? The last we heard, the International Red Cross had a pretty good handle on the situation up there.''

The general nodded grimly and said, ''That is what we just told Mexico. El Presidente Diaz seems to wish for to help us anyway.''

Gaston asked, ''Don't you mean he wants to help himself to some of Guatemala, Mon General?''

The Guatemalan officer sighed and said, ''Your dossier says you are familiar with Mexican political aspirations, Lieutenant Verrier. As you know, Diaz has somehow managed to convince Washington he is a, how you say, benevolent despot, friendly to the United States. The ruling junta here in Guatemala, alas, is considered a military dictatorship.''

"Isn't it?" asked Gaston, before Captain Gringo could kick him.

The general shrugged and said, "Few nations south of the Rio Bravo are governed as democratically as idealistic Americans or even French might wish. Let us make no bones about it. Guatemala is, as they say, a military dictatorship. We *tried* democracy for a time, after we threw the Spanish out. It simply isn't practical in a country where ninety percent of the people neither read nor write, and many do not even speak Spanish. Our barefoot campesinos and their Indio cousins in the jungles and chaparral are not ready for democracy. Meanwhile, we few educated people offer them reasonable justice and prosperity, earthquakes and invading armies permitting."

Captain Gringo said, "You don't have to sell us on the idea your government's a big improvement on Mexico's, Sir. Gaston and I met on the wrong side of a Mexican firing squad one time, and neither of us had done a damned thing to rate so much attention!"

The general looked relieved and said, "Bueno. I have read about the way you helped a handful of our soldados up by Boca Bruja and I was most favorably impressed by that, as well. If I gave you a regiment of cavalry, with a heavy-weapons troop and a battery of mountain artillery, do you think you could, ah, discourage the Mexicans from trying to be so nice to us? Obviously I can't commision two notorious soldiers of fortune as Guatemalan regular officers. But you will have unofficial brevet ranks, and under-the-table pay, of course, to go with the duties of colonel and lieutenant colonel.

Captain Gringo whistled softly and said, "You must need officers pretty badly, sir! What happened to all your regular field-grade guys?"

The general grimaced and said, "Almost all my top men

are members of either the Barrios or the Cabrera faction. Need I say more?''

Captain Gringo shook his head. Gaston said, ''Eh, bien, until you high-ranking junta members find out which faction is plotting what, you wish to keep them where you can keep a très jaundiced eye on them, hein?''

The general shrugged and said, ''We most certainly do not intend to entrust anyone below the rank of brigadier with that much military power until we know for certain he can be *trusted*! As you may have heard, the *heads* of the Barrios and Cabrera families are in complete agreement, but also completely in the dark about this rumor of a plot to make one clan or the other dominant. Until we find out just what is going on among the lower ranks, we have agreed to keep the balance of power balanced indeed. Since neither of you have any connection with either family, and since few if any native Guatemalan soldados would follow orders from a foreigner to fight their own country, we are faced with the frankly grotesque choice of entrusting our border defenses to outside mercenaries or just letting that unwashed bastard, Diaz, *have* our northwest provinces!''

Gaston chuckled and said that sounded ''très pratique.'' But Captain Gringo asked, ''Isn't it possible, Sir, that Mexico started all this shit about a family feud, just to castrate your army while Diaz was plotting his power play?''

The general sighed and said, ''We've thought of that. We hope it's true. Meanwhile, we can't take chances. You saw up at the Barrios house this morning that whatever is going on is serious indeed!''

Captain Gringo nodded and said, ''Yeah, not many bush-league plotters get to plot with four-pounder field guns. Has your army intelligence gotten a line on who those guys might have been, or where they got the big gun?''

The general shook his head and said, "The irregular gun crew was in no condition to talk, thanks to you two. Not that I would have handled the situation any differently. One still shudders to consider what might have happened had they fired *over* that house into the city below! The gun was British army surplus. And old model no longer made. God knows how it got to Central America. Perhaps from the so-called British Crown Colony to the east. None of our own artillery units are missing any ordnance and, in any case, we don't use that model."

"Has anyone come up with any notion as to why Evita Barrios was the intended target, sir? She told me earlier that she had relatives on both sides."

The general nodded and said, "She does, and both sides would have been most outraged had a pretty young kinswoman been blown out of bed by a cannon shell!"

Gaston tried to cover a sleepy yawn with his cigar. But their host caught it and said, "Forgive me, Señores. I know you have both been up all night, and what an exciting night you had! Why do you not sleep on my offer and we can work out the details later in the day, should you accept the mission?"

Neither soldier of fortune was dumb enough to ask what happened if they refused. So, when they both nodded, the general rang a bell on his desk, and when the same aide came in he told him to show Captain Gringo and Gaston to their new quarters. They shook on it with him and parted friendly.

But naturally, as soon as they were alone in adjoining rooms in the upstairs BOQ, Gaston shut the door leading out to the corridor and asked, "Do we make a break for it now, or after we get some sleep?"

Captain Gringo growled, "Neither," as he glanced around the Spartan but comfortable chamber they'd issued him. The walls of course were stucco over heavy masonry. The furnish-

ings were army issue, save for the bed, which was a big
four-poster a lot more yummy-looking than he'd ever seen in
a U.S. Army BOQ. But one of the few things he liked about
soldiering this far south was that Latin American officers saw
no need to show the world how tough they were by doing
without all the comforts of home.

He said, "Look, we're professional soldiers and the old
man's offered us a better-than-average deal. For a change
we'll have regular troops to command instead of ragged-ass
guerrillas. The enemy is clear-cut. So we don't have to worry
about shooting pigs and chickens for the usual piss-pot
dictatorship. What do you want, egg in your *cerveza?*"

Gaston said, "I want to get back to Costa Rica *alive*. I
agree that shooting Mexican federales is a service to humani-
ty in general. But this sneaky political situation makes me
très nervous, Dick! How do we know the men who wish to
hire us will still be in power when and if we get back?"

Captain Gringo said, "Unless I'm a piss-poor judge of
character, that old general figures to keep his four stars
awhile. His whole point in contracting with outside help is
that he's a sly old dog who keeps his back to the wall and
covers all bets. Hell, if he was *dumb,* he'd put officers from
his own faction in command of the expedition. But until he
knows what's going on, and who figures to win, he's not
trusting his own brothers!"

Gaston said, "I don't trust them, or him, either. But since I
can't persuade you to elope with me, or even bend over, I'm
going to bed."

He did so, slamming the door between their adjoining
rooms. Captain Gringo chuckled, made sure the hall door was
locked, and got undressed. He put his .38 under the pillows,
on safe. Then, though he was tired as hell, he took the time
to give himself a quick whore bath with a washcloth at the

washstand in the corner. He needed a shave, too, but that could wait. He slid between the clean cotton sheets and was asleep in no time. But some of the dreams his worried mind dredged up from the past forty-eight hours were pissers.

Pantera was chasing him down an endless corridor with a jar of hot salve in one hand and a sheet of sandpaper in the other when he realized that the repeated knocking he kept hearing wasn't part of his dream and woke up. The sunlight through the window blinds was painting tiger stripes on the far wall and doorway at an angle that told him he'd been asleep at least four or five hours. Whoever was out in the hallway knocked again. So he said, "Sí, sí, un momento," and swung his naked feet to the tile floor. He stood up, grabbed a towel from the washstand in passing, and wrapped it around his hips as he gripped the .38 casually in its knot and opened the door with his free hand.

He was glad he'd thought to grab the towel. He'd assumed the old general had sent a male officer for him, even if it was nearly siesta time. But his visitors were dames. Three of them. They all crowded in at once, as one of them explained with a giggle, "We do not wish for to be seen coming in, Deek."

"You know my name?" he asked with a puzzled smile.

Another said, "Sí, you are Deek Walker, the famous Captain Gringo, and we are so honored."

He asked them to what he owed the honor of their unexpected visit as he looked them over. All three were pretty and dressed peon in low-cut blouses and bright print peasant skirts. But that was the only real resemblance. One was a willowy mulatto with coffee-and-cream skin and a rose in her not-quite-kinky hair. Another was a plumper mestiza with her

Indian-straight black hair in braids. The other was poor-white with wavy dark red hair and features that betrayed a wayward Irish beachcomber somewhere in her family tree, although she seemed mostly Hispanic.

She was the one who announced, with a brazen smile, "We are of course the adelitas who go with your position, Captain Gringo. I am Carmella. Allow me to present Elena y Alicia!"

He laughed and said, "I've heard of rank having its privileges, but this can't be good for discipline! I hope you muchachas won't take me for a sissy, but I wasn't planning on taking *any* women out in the field against the Mexican army!"

The mulatto, Alicia, asked, "Why not? We are regular army."

The mestiza, Elena, said, "If you wish for to march against los federales with no women along, you will find yourself marching *alone,* Querido! Our men do not campaign very well with unsatisfied erections!"

He sighed and muttered, "I've noticed that, down here. Are you ladies really on the army payroll?"

The redhead nodded and said, "Sí, as nurses and laundresses, on the books. The three of us have been, how you say, on extended leave since the colonel who used to command this regiment died almost a year ago."

"I can see how army life injured his health. He had all *three* of you, ah, doing his laundry?"

The mulatto laughed lewdly and proceeded to undress as she said, "He was a good man while he lasted. But for why are we all in this ridiculous vertical position? None of us have had any sex for months and we have the whole siesta ahead of us for to catch up!"

As she threw her tawny naked body across Captain Gringo's rumpled sheets, the redhead protested, "Alicia, that is not fair!" as the little plump mestiza, obviously a pragmatic child, shucked her own clothes to offer Captain Gringo a better view of what *she* had to offer. She had a lot. He was uncomfortably aware of how the towel around his middle was starting to bulge as Elena joined her naked rival on the bed, and the redhead, stamping her foot in annoyance, began to peel her own clothes off, saying, "You two are cheating, dammit! I thought we agreed to let him choose between us fair and square!"

Captain Gringo laughed again as he got the picture, which was sure starting to get dirty. As Carmella stepped out of her fallen skirts, allowing him to see. that she was a redhead all over, he said, "Oh, that sounds more reasonable. Your old CO only had to take you on one at a time, right?"

Carmella stepped closer, smiling down at the bulge under his towel, as she said, "Sí; it is up to you to choose which one of us you want first. I am the best in bed. Colonel Barrios always said so."

There was a wail of protest from the bed as both the mulatto and the mestiza tried to convince him that she was full of shit. But Carmella had the strategic advantage of being on her feet and closest to Captain Gringo. So she put her bare arms around him and proceeded to grind her ruddy little bush against the terry cloth between them. The towel didn't stay there long. He hung on to the .38 but let the towel fall anywhere it had a mind to as he held Carmella closer with his free hand, but said, "Hold the thought, Querida. I don't want any of you ladies to feel left out. But this is going to call for some ingenuity. As you can see, I don't have three of these things, much as I'd like to take all three of you on at once!"

The redhead reached down to take the matter in question in hand as she backed toward the rather crowded bed, saying,

"Finders keepers! If you are man enough for all three of us, there is no real problem!"

So the next thing he knew he was in bed with three giggling girls and getting kissed all over as he suddenly found himself inside at least one of them as he kissed Carmella, assuming it was she. But, though she kissed him back, with passion, as he started moving faster in what he'd taken to be she, she complained, "Elena, you bitch! How did you get your Indian cunt around my man's cock?"

Captain Gringo was damned if he knew, either, but when he craned his neck to look, he saw the brown-skinned mestiza's belly against his, as Carmella's whiter hips bumped against Elena's in frustration. The mulatto, Alicia, had meanwhile moved around to kiss and tongue his bounding buttocks as she played with his scrotum. He laughed and asked Carmella to move over a bit and let him finish right with Elena, adding, "I promise you're next, all right?"

Alicia bit him in mock savagery on one cheek of his rump, protesting, "That's not fair! I've been helping you come the most!" as little brown Elena, now that the redhead was partly out of the way, put her arms around Captain Gringo and hugged him to her firm brown breasts, observing, "That is not true, Alicia. I am doing the most to make him come with my insides and . . . Ay. caramba, *I* am coming, too, with his big carazo filling me so nicely!"

He could tell she was telling the truth as her vaginal walls contracted on his pounding shaft. But the little mestiza was sneaky and kept murmuring she was *about* to come when he knew for a fact she had already. The redhead whimpered, "Hurry, hurry, I am so hot I can't stand it! Alicia, are you as hot as I?"

"Hotter!" the mulatto said with a giggle as Captain Gringo went on pounding Elena, not wanting to take it out until he'd enjoyed her fully at least once, and cooled enough by the wild situation to take longer than he might have. It was distracting to make love to one total stranger in broad daylight with two naked women he'd never had watching. But as he tried to let himself go with the mestiza, the other two stopped watching him and Elena. He found it even more distracting when the redhead and the willowy dark Alicia proceeded to go sixty-nine right next to him on the same bouncing mattress. Alicia's chocolate rump was closest to his head and he sort of regretted his promise to Carmella when he saw what the roguish redhead was licking with her darting tongue. He turned to the girl he was laying and asked conversationally, "Do they go in for that often?"

Elena smiled dreamily, gripping tightly with her internal muscles as she replied, with no hint of embarrassment, "Sí. We are not allowed to make love to any man but the soldado we have been assigned to, and, up until now, we have never had such a virile commanding officer!"

He didn't answer. He was almost there, himself, as she came again in his arms. So he kissed Elena and let himself go as, beside him, the redhead sobbed and said, "Oh, faster, Alicia, do it faster, I am comingggggg!"

Apparently all four of them did about the same time. For as he finished ejaculating in Elena and went limp atop her, he saw that the white and the black girl beside them had collapsed in a contented angle of contrasting limbs as well.

But a promise was a promise. So as he withdrew from Elena he laughed and said, "Get your head out of Carmella's lap, Alicia. I think it's her turn, right?"

But the redhead on the bottom sobbed. "Wait, I wish for to be eaten some more. I know it is vile, but once I start coming that way I just can't get enough!"

He said that sounded fair as he rolled onto his hands and

knees to get in position behind the mulatto and enter her dog-style as she hissed in delight with her mouth still filled with moist red thatch.

Captain Gringo hissed with delight, too. For the slenderer dark hips of Alicia held pleasures between them that felt as nice as they'd looked while he was laying Elena. Carmella's head was still on the sheets between the mulatto's widespread thighs, of course, and as she stared directly up at what was happening right above her, Carmella gasped and said, "Oh, God, I didn't know what I was missing! But don't stop eating me, you black bitch! This is so exciting!"

Alicia found it exciting too, from the way she was moving her dark hips to meet his thrusts as she made perverse love to another woman who, in turn, teased them both with skilled fingers and giggling comments on the way it looked to her from down there. The mulatto came up for air and gasped as she said, "Elena, take over for me with Carmella, por favor. I see what you mean about this one and I wish for to do it *right* with him!"

Actually, Captain Gringo had no complaints about the way they'd been doing it so far. But he changed his mind when the slender mulatto rolled off for a moment and faced him, smiling up at him, on her back, as the redhead and the mestiza started going at it lesbian. He dropped into the welcoming saddle of Alicia's chocolate thighs and lay atop her smaller but firmer dark breasts to give it to her old-fashioned. He wasn't sure he wanted to kiss lips that had just been down on another lady, until he found out how swell Alicia kissed and figured, what the hell, it wasn't like she'd been down on a *man*, after all. He could see how Carmella must have enjoyed oral sex with the mulatto, once Alicia showed him how amazingly long her tongue was. She held him close and didn't stop kissing him passionately until he felt her coming and returned the compliment by ejaculating in her, too. He would have been willing to keep going, in anything so nice, but Alicia was either fair-minded or, more likely, a lady who liked variety. Because she laughed, low and dirty, and said, "He's all yours, Carmella. I can assure you you'll find he was worth waiting for!"

The redhead untangled herself from her bisexual mestiza partner and changed places with Alicia, as all Captain Gringo had to do was to raise himself to his hands and knees to make room for the interesting switch. But as he found himself staring down at paler and fuller curves where Alicia's darker thinner charms had just been, he hoped he was still man enough to service yet another partner. Both the girls he'd just had had been good enough to satisfy most any man, and he'd had two *other* women in the past twenty-four hours.

But as the redhead took him in her arms, and everywhere else, he saw that he had nothing to worry about. He'd thought she was just bragging when she'd said the late Colonel Barrios had said she was the best.

Having had the guy's wife as well, if they were talking about the same Colonel Barrios, Captain Gringo had to admit that the old bastard had known what he was talking about. The hot-blooded redhead wasn't simply sex crazy. She made love in a way to drive *him* crazy, and he was glad he'd saved her for last. He never would have been able to satisfy anything this tight and overactive had he not had a couple of practice runs to calm his nerves. He hardly had to move his hips at all as Carmella literally sucked him off with her rippling internal muscles. But the little moving he did seemed to please her immensely, judging from the way she kept bragging about her protracted and repeated orgasms, while the other two just tongued each other to distraction without comment.

He finally came, and just lay there in her entwining limbs as she milked his sated shaft with her skilled vagina. He tried to remember if the somewhat prettier Evita had felt this yummy after they'd come together up on the ridge the night before.

She'd said her husband had been a virile old goat. That was for damned sure, if he'd cheated on such a pretty young wife with these three oversexed peon adelitas. He wondered if Evita had known, and if she'd been faithful to the colonel whether she'd known or not. He knew *these* three hadn't been faithful to a dirty old man's memory for anything like a year, no matter what they said. No dame who screwed so good, including Evita, come to think of it, was about to go close to a year without at least a little practice to keep her skills up.

He felt his limp shaft being extruded by Carmella's continued contractions, and rolled off, since there was no point in trying to show off to such an obvious old pro. He kissed her disappointed Mona Lisa smile, to be polite, and said, "Take ten. Smoke 'em if you got 'em. We're going to have to work this out a bit more sensibly, muchachas. I have to *lead* the regiment to meet the Mexicans. I don't want to have to be *carried* into battle. Now that we're all old friends, I think we'd better limit me to one lady per siesta and/or rest stop. Obviously the two left out can find something to occupy their time. That's assuming, of course, I can't talk you into, ah, sort of sharing the wealth. I have a partner next door who likes girls a lot and . . ."

"Your little French friend *has* his adelitas," Carmella cut in, reaching for his limpness as she added, "Holding the brevet rank of lieutenant colonel, he only rates *two* adelitas in this man's army. But two ought to be enough for to satisfy such an elderly person, no?"

Captain Gringo laughed and said, "I was wondering why

things were so quiet next door. The only times Gaston ever shuts up is when he's sleeping or his mouth is full. Okay, if I'm stuck with the three of you, I'll just have to be brave, I guess. But, no estercolar, muchachas, we're going to have to be more sensible in the future. I'll tell you what. Each day on the trail the three of you can decide between you whose turn it is. That way, I'll wind up pleasantly surprised and won't have to insult anyone."

The two going sixty-nine giggled in agreement. The redhead said, "We'll worry about that later. We are not on the trail *now*. We have the rest of la siesta for to get to know each other better, no?"

"Jesus, how much better can I get to know any of you? Cut it out, Carmella. I'm really bushed!"

But, as she'd foreseen, he didn't stay bushed long, as the redhead rolled her head in his lap to swallow him alive. So he leaned back with a bemused smile and murmured, "Oh, well, since you put it *that* way."

Their cavalry regiment looked pretty spiffy when Captain Gringo and Gaston inspected it, dismounted, on the parade later that afternoon. The two soldiers of fortune were walking sort of funny but otherwise looked pretty spiffy, too, in the quasi-officer's kit they'd been issued before leaving their assigned quarters and diamond patrol of adelitas. But neither wore any indication of rank, and as they moved down the line they noticed that nobody under their command now wore anything on his khakis indicating any official connection with the regular army of Guatemala.

The general had explained that should anyone be killed or captured by the officially friendly Mexican federales, Guatemala would have no idea who they might have been. On paper it was true, perhaps, that a cavalry patrol had been sent to scout for the notorious rebel leader Caballero Blanco, no matter what the papers might say about him being sort of dead. But said cavalry troops had official orders not to tangle with their friendly neighbors to the north. So the *unofficial* command of Captain Gringo had been ordered to leave all pay books and ID in the safe at GHQ and told that they'd be paid, promoted, and decorated if and when they got back from a successful mission.

The general hadn't said so, but everyone knew better than to come back at all if they screwed up.

Each unit of the regiment of course had its own low-ranking officers, none of them named Barrios or Cabrera, and none wearing any indication of rank. The troopers knew who they were supposed to take orders from and it was none of El Presidente Diaz's business.

The highest native rank was invisibly held by a Captain Martinez, commanding the heavy-weapons troop. Captain Gringo spent the most time inspecting them. Martinez and his boys had a battery of out-of-date Gatling guns and two more reasonable Maxim machine guns mounted on the same dumb little gun carriages. All the heavy weapons had been chambered for the same .30-30 rounds as the troopers' carbines, and Captain Gringo noted with approval that Martinez kept his weapons spit and polish with proper headspacing. So he made Martinez his regimental adjutant to cheer him up, and decided he'd tell him later that they'd be leaving the Gatlings behind and packing the machine guns without the silly wheels.

Gaston was less favorably impressed by the mountain artillery battery attached to the expedition. The little smooth-bore muzzle loaders were more out-of-date than the guns he'd fought the Prussians with back in '70, and France, merde alors, had *lost!*

Gaston cursed even louder when he inspected the battery's ammo. Since it was a dismounted inspection, the mountain guns and their ammo caissons were set up on their removable wheels. Gaston broke open a caisson and, after calling a red-faced gunnery sergeant the son of a one-legged harelipped whore, asked him what in the name of le bon Dieu he called this species of merde in what was supposed to be an artillery caisson. The sergeant protested that it was ammo. Gaston told him his mother was a syphilitic camel as well as ugly and added, "*You* may call this ammunition. I call it grape and canister left over from the Battle of Waterloo! Don't we have any exploding shells at all?"

"This is all they issued us, Señor. But, as you see, we have plenty of propellant charges."

"Eh bien, to propel *what*? These adorable antiques have about the same range as my spit, and they can lob a projectile no bigger than a tomato can. Do you really expect me to fire point-blank at charging Mexican cavalry with Napoleonic beanbags?"

"I think the *general* does, Señor."

Gaston said he'd like to be excused for the rest of the afternoon. Captain Gringo, who'd been listening and had other worries, told him to cut the comedy, adding, "We have to get within *range* of the fucking Mexicans before we have to worry about *shooting* any of them. Take over and dismiss the troops but tell 'em not to leave the post. I've got some other nits to pick with the general."

He turned away and grumped over to GHQ, where he found the old man and some other junta officers seated around a table on the veranda, playing dominoes. The general asked if he'd like to sit in. Captain Gringo said, "No, thank you, Sir. I haven't time. I'd like to move the outfit out just after sunset but, ah, could I speak to you alone, Sir?"

The general shook his head and said, "We are all friends here. You may speak freely, Captain Gringo."

But before he could, one of the other old farts asked, "Do you think it wise to leave after dark, Captain Gringo? The men we gave you to lead are all well-chosen volunteers, but none of them are trained as night fighters. It is not our custom for to march at night down here."

Captain Gringo nodded and said, "I know that, Colonel. That's why I'd like to move them off post under cover of darkness. Mexico has to have at least *one* spy wandering around Guatemala City by now."

The general chuckled fondly and observed, "I told you all he was a clever young man. You may leave whenever you wish, Captain Gringo. But is that all you wished to consult me about?"

"Nosir. Gaston and me have tangled with the Mexican federales before. They're good. Damned good. If you expect me to even slow them down with a light cav regiment, I'm going to have to hit them hard and often in hit-and-run skirmishes. I don't have the weight to take on even one of what Diaz calls a federale regiment. He packs more riders in a troop and backs them with heavy modern artillery. I don't know why Uncle Sam arms Mexico so well, either, but he does. If I allow myself and your men to wind up pinned down, los federales have to win."

"Our men are braver than any mother-loving Mexicans!" a portly junta officer protested indignantly.

Captain Gringo nodded and said, "I'm sure they are, Sir. But brave doesn't count when a twelve-pounder goes off under your balls. So I want to keep my people moving around too fast for enemy artillery to range on their positions."

"We're sure you can," soothed the general, placing another domino on the table in front of him, with more attention than he was giving the worried American.

Captain Gringo said, "I just inspected the men. They look okay. But I understand we're expected to take along at least one adelita for every man in the regiment?"

The general smiled and said, "They are not *all* adelitas. Some of the troopers will be bringing their own wives along. No children, of course. One must draw the limit somewhere, no?"

Captain Gringo grimaced and said, "With your permission, Sir, I'd like to leave the women behind."

The general looked up at him, bemused, and said, "Surely you jest?"

Another junta officer laughed and said, "It is not difficult to *order* men to do anything. The problem is getting them to *do* it. This is the Guatemalan Army, Señor, not a celibate organization of fighting monks!"

The general nodded and said, "The women never do what they are told in any case. You would have more trouble with both your men and their women than the added mobility would be worth, Captain Gringo."

The big Yank shrugged and said, "I guess you're right, Sir. But if we have to drag the dames along, what sort of mounts can we provide for them?"

The general looked sincerely puzzled as he asked, "Mounts? What mounts? Who ever heard of mounted adelitas? It is the accepted task of the women attached to an army to keep up as best they can, on foot."

Another officer nodded and said, "Sí; cavalry on the move travels mostly at a walk, and nobody expects the women and other baggage for to join in any cavalry charges, eh?"

Captain Gringo swore under his breath and said, "I was afraid that was the way this army worked it, too. Señores, if you expect me to play hit-and-run with los federales in the chaparral of the border country, you're going to have to let me mount everyone connected with the expedition. I *won't* be moving at a walk up there. I'm hoping los federales will. We can't hope to even *worry* the bastards unless we're in shape to bounce around them like spit on a hot stove, and I'm not about to camp in one spot long enough for them to get the range on us with their bigger guns. So, if the women have to come along, they'll have to come along mounted, and *armed!*''

The general frowned and muttered, ''Armed adelitas? Is that allowed under the rules of civilized warfare, Captain Gringo?''

The American shook his head and said, ''Nosir. Any of them captured by the Mexicans will probably be shot as irregulars, after being raped, of course. But what's the difference? Los federales rape and shoot all female prisoners in any case!''

The general nodded and said, ''Es verdad. I see you *do* know the methods of our old friend Diaz. Very well, you have my permiso to issue arms and horses to the, ah, dependents of your expedition.''

Captain Gringo said, ''That's another thing I wanted to ask about, General. I'm an old cavalry man myself. So I know how cavalry troopers feel about mules. But I want mules anyway.''

''Of course you will have mules.'' The general nodded, adding, ''For to pack the heavy weapons and, if you like, the adelitas and other baggage.''

Captain Gringo shook his head and said, ''I want mules for *everyone,* Sir. I know the country to the north. Gaston and I just came down here through a lot of it, and it's rough as hell. Good Spanish mules have the edge on horses in rough dry country and we'll need all the edge we can get.''

An older officer on the far side of the table gasped in dismay and asked, "Are you loco en la cabeza? Whoever heard of crack cavalry riding into battle aboard *mules*, for God's sake?"

"El Cid and the other Spanish knights who drove the Moors out of Castile, if you want to look it up in the history books, Colonel. The Moors made the mistake of riding Arab chargers into the high, dry central mountains of Iberia, where the water holes were few and far between and the trails were steep and treacherous. The Spanish cavalry didn't look as *pretty*, riding against them on lop-eared, surefooted mules. But we all know who won in the end. Los federales like to look pretty too, and they'll have their own adelitas packing the baggage behind their Arabs and Spanish barbs, on foot. So they'll have to move slow and they'll have to beeline through the chaparral for the little fodder and water to be found up that way."

He would have said more, but the general hadn't gotten to be a general by being a stupid man. So he nodded and cut in, "Bueno. I told you when I recruited you that you were free to do things your own way. But the men are not going to understand or like your methods, I'm afraid."

Captain Gringo smiled grimly and replied, "Where in the articles of war does it say soldiers are supposed to understand or like their orders, Sir? As long as I have *your* permission to make a few changes, I'd better get cracking and have the outfit ready to move out by sundown."

The troopers didn't understand or like Captain Gringo's changes at all, and nine hundred men muttering curses as they trotted their new mounts by moonlight added up to quite a mutter indeed. But Captain Gringo, at the head of the column, let them vent their spleen without comment for the moment. Good soldiers always griped. The women riding with them giggled a lot instead of cursing. They were delighted to be riding even mules, for a change, albeit somewhat confused about the saddle guns they'd been issued. Captain Gringo had told each soldado not to load his adelita's carbine until he'd had time to instruct her some about which end the bullets came out. He'd made each man in the outfit personally responsible for his own woman's military training and he'd warned them what would happen if a dame shot anyone on their side, by accident or because it was that time of the month.

More than one of them was sure a maniac was leading them all to their doom, and kept saying so, as he led them at a mile-eating but uncomfortable trot across the farmlands north of Guatemala City, hoping to be well clear of them by the time anyone who liked to gossip was out in the field chopping weeds.

Gaston had left his disassembled mountain artillery aboard its own pack mules in the care of the gunnery sergeant who thought *he* was crazy, too. So the sardonic Frenchman was riding with Captain Gringo and Martinez when the moon started winking off and on. Some idiot riding behind them shouted that it was going to start raining any minute, as if nobody else in the outfit could figure that out for him- or herself. Captain Gringo called back, "Keep it down to a roar, dammit. Let the Mexicans figure out we're coming. Don't tell the whole fucking world about it!"

Martinez looked up at the gathering clouds and observed, "We are going to get most wet before morning, unless we stop for to pitch our tents, Captain Gringo."

The taller American said, "Bueno. It's hard to count

passing troops when the rain keeps you indoors. We're not about to stop for anything until we're clear of civilization, Martinez. Haven't you got a poncho?''

''Sí; but one always gets wet anyway, riding through a real storm, and those clouds *promise* one!''

Captain Gringo shrugged and said, ''Tough shit. Gaston, you know your way around these parts better than me. How far do we have to make it by sunrise if we don't want some farm kids coming over to bum tobacco off us?''

Gaston said, ''I don't know, Dick. I haven't ridden this way since back in eighty-five, and I can't believe how it's changed. We must be close to eight or ten miles out of the city by now, and when the world was younger, this open country was less open. Someone with a machete has been cutting a lot of firewood around here, non?''

Martinez, trying to be a good sport, said, ''*I* can remember when it was more wooded this far from town, too, Señores. When I was a boy we used to hunt in thick woods, just a short walk out into the hills. At the rate our people are clearing the land, the whole country will be open brushland in a few more years. I read in a book by a professor that this is bad for the land. I believe it. But what else can our people do? They must have fuel for to cook with, and Guatemala has no oil or coal.''

Gaston said, ''I would not worry about it. There is still more than enough jungle for me in your très soggy if attractive country. I am glad we are not being sent northeast instead of northwest. The high country ahead is dismal enough. Trying to lead a regiment of women and children through the lowland jungle would be très fatigué indeed!''

A raindrop big enough to float a modest goldfish plopped down on the beak of Captain Gringo's military kepi. So it sounded pretty dumb to him when Martinez said, "Dammit, here comes the rain."

Not even Gaston had to tell him he was right as the sky opened up and dumped buckets of spit-warm tropic rain on them. Martinez went through the motions of putting on his poncho. Neither Captain Gringo nor Gaston bothered. They were all soaking wet before anyone born of mortal woman could have done anything constructive about it.

But he knew mules would take less crap off an officer than his human followers would. So he raised his free hand and called out, "Caminar!" to slow the column to a slow but steady walk that would rest the mules and hopefully take less rain under kepi peaks or sombrero brims.

Carmella was wearing a straw sombrero over her dark red hair as she caught up with him aboard her own steaming mule to call out, "Deek, it is raining and we are getting wet!"

Captain Gringo said, "That sounds like one of those Japanese haiku poems, and it makes about as important a point, Carmella. You know I think you're pretty. But adelitas are not supposed to ride at the head of the column."

She insisted, "Deek, the others are saying bad things about you. Some of the other girls are talking about turning back."

He said, "I sure hope you're right, Doll. I've never led one of these suffragette demonstrations before. Pass the word that I won't say a thing if the ladies want to keep their mounts. But tell 'em to leave the guns and ammo with their soldados."

Carmella said, "Deek, you do not understand. If an adelita refuses for to go on, her soldado will desert as well!"

He said, "Not if he doesn't want to stand against a wall he won't. Pass the word that I haven't got time to chase deserters. But tell 'em to just remember GHQ has their pay books and home addresses on file."

Carmella observed that some adelitas could be very convincing, but dropped back, anyway, when he repeated the order. Martinez, riding on his other side, said, "She could be right, I fear. Discipline is not as tight as it should be in this army, alas."

Captain Gringo shrugged and said, "I've noticed that lately. You always have to figure on some desertion at a time like this. Many a guy who's willing to soldier in a comfy garrison tends to have some second thoughts when he finds himself out in the field where things can go boomp in the night. Let's hope we separate the men from the boys poco tiempo. It's better to get the bad apples out of the barrel early in the game. Closer to the enemy, they can be a real problem."

Martinez frowned thoughtfully and said, "I can follow your logic to a point, Captain Gringo. But how many men can we afford to lose?"

The taller-in-the-saddle American grimaced and said, "A couple of troops of real fighters can carve up a division of half-assed slackers, in a pinch. Don't forget, Mexico drafts almost anyone who can walk, and they don't *let* unwilling fighters fall out by the wayside."

Gaston, who'd been listening, said, "Let us not get overly optimistic, Dick. You forget I served as a Mexican officer in my misspent youth. It is true an illiterate peon kidnapped on his wedding day by a press gang makes a poor recruit. But los federales *do* go in for discipline, and the survivors of their très draconian basic training tend to soldier well indeed. Some of your Texas friends learned that the hard way, at a place called the Alamo, non?"

Captain Gringo smiled thinly and said, "That was a little before my time. But this won't be the first time I've tangled with los federales. I figure their cavalry screen will be pretty good. But if they're really pushing a railroad through the chaparral, like the general said, we'll be mostly up against an engineer brigade. I doubt they'll have much training with anything but picks and shovels.''

Gaston said, ''True. No Mexican engineering officer with any brains would want a forced laborer armed with a *gun* anywhere near him. But to rip up their adorable tracks, we still have to punch through the screen of cavalry you just cheered me so by mentioning. Take it from one who knows, Mexican cavalry is *good!*''

''We'll just have to be better, then,'' said Captain Gringo dryly, as he led his column on through the pouring rain.

Meanwhile, back at GHQ, the general was getting wet, too, even though he was under the tile roof of his comfortable quarters. He was soaking the sheets and the lady on them, under him, with sweat, as he tried in vain to ejaculate in her. But, as the dentures in the glass by the side of the bed and his corset hanging over the foot of it might indicate, the general was getting a little old and flabby for twice in one night, even with a partner so young and understanding.

Pantera, who'd told the general to call her Lolita, was getting bored with looking at the ceiling while a sweaty old fool wiggled a far-from-filling expectation in her skilled but lukewarm interior. But she chose her words delicately, not wanting to bruise an old man's delicate ego, as she said with mock enthusiasm, ''Oh, let me get on top, Querido! You have me so excited I can't stand it. But I wish for to try something naughty.''

The old man rolled off with a sigh of relief and gratitude to the aide who'd introduced him to such an understanding and pretty playmate. She certainly was a hairy little thing, he noticed once more, as the beautiful but somewhat Neanderthal Pantera sat up in bed to wipe her hairy nippled breasts and fuzzy belly dry with a corner of the top sheet. The general lay back expectantly. She gave fantastic face, as he recalled from earlier in the evening when she'd gotten it up for him in the first place. He said, "Bueno, let us do it in the French manner while I get my second wind, Querida."

But Pantera laughed teasingly and said, "I wish for to try a new thrill. You promise you won't think me perverse? I don't do funny things with just *any* man I meet, you know. But you are so handsome, and you seem to be such a man of the world."

"Oh, I am, I *am!*" the general assured her, hoping against hope that the little spitfire really did know something new to him. The general had been used to having his way with women for a very long time, and, in his time, he had tried everything that didn't hurt and, more than once, something that did. Like many a spoiled old man, his appetite was all too often bigger than his stomach.

Pantera climbed atop her elderly patient, facing the foot of the bed, with her shapely albeit hairy rear view presented to him as she reached down to take his wilted flower of manhood in hand. He watched, bemused, as she stroked him back to life with her amazingly skilled fingers. Even without eucalyptus salve Pantera could hold a man's undivided attention and, if he was still breathing at all, get it up for him. So the general started breathing faster as he feasted his eyes on her fuzzy tail bone and the hairy slit below it, saying, "Enough, Lolita! For God's sake, put it in right before you get your pretty little palm all wet with wasted joy!"

She giggled coyly and rose just enough to position his shaft before settling down on it to sigh, "Oh, it feels so big this way!"

The general blinked in surprise, albeit not dismay, as he realized where she was taking it. Anal entry was no great novelty to a high-ranking officer accustomed to being served by willing love slaves, of course. (As a lower-ranking officer he'd had to *take* it in the ass more than once.) But she did feel much tighter back there, and the almost-masculine hairiness of her otherwise feminine hourglass aroused perverse and hence intriguing feelings in the jaded old man as she started moving up and down, playing with his testes with her hands at the same time.

She asked if he liked it, faking more interest in his silly little tool than she really felt as she contracted her anal muscles on it with the skilled detachment of the professional she was. Like most really successful whores, Pantera, when serving a customer, felt no more for him than a barber felt for the hair he was cutting. But, like a good barber, she prided herself on good service. The poor old man's little wee-wee in her ass thrilled her, and filled her, hardly more than if she'd been wiping it hard after going to the toilet. She sensed that the damned fool thing was still half-soft inside her and, hell, how long was she supposed to toil for her pay like this? She leaned forward, letting him have a better view of himself as she slid her pink rectal rim up and down it. Then, bracing her weight on one hand, Pantera licked the fingers of the other and, holding his scrotum in her palm, slid first one and then two fingers up the general's surprised anal opening.

He gasped. "Ay caramba! What are you doing to my ass, you naughty child?"

Pantera laughed lewdly as she proceeded to give him a prostate massage that jerked his shaft to full erection inside her own rectum. He gasped again as he said, "Faster! Oh, Jesus, move *faster*, Lolita!"

But she didn't. She knew what she was doing better than he did. She settled back on him, taking him all the way up inside her and clamping tight as she massaged the roots of his remaining virility with skill and vigor, until, as she knew it would, the old man's confused and perversely stimulated sex organ exploded in a way that nearly knocked him out.

She laughed and said, "Oh, I felt that, and *I* came, too, you naughty boy! Do you still wish for to go French with me?"

"Uh, not under the present circumstances, my dear. Couldn't we just rest a bit for now?"

Pantera sighed in mock disappointment and slid off, wiping her customer thoughtfully with another corner of the sheet before snuggling down beside him to tell him how great he was, again.

The general patted her fuzzy shoulder fondly and suppressed a yawn as he agreed, modestly, that most women found him muy toro for a man his age.

Pantera knew he wanted to fall asleep. So it was about time to strike. She snuggled closer and murmured, "I only wish you had more time for poor little me. But you are such a busy man these days."

"That's true." The general sighed, half-asleep. It had been a most busy day. But now he'd enjoyed a warm meal and come twice, for God's sake, in the wildest woman he'd had for ages. So why was he still awake?

Pantera asked, keeping her voice casual and drowsy, "Was that dispatch your aide handed you in the hall as we were coming up here anything I have to worry about, Querido? I mean, military matters are of no great interest to poor little me, but I do hope you will not have to go out in the field soon, now that we have *found* each other."

The general yawned and said, "Don't worry, Lolita. Generals are not expected for to lead expeditions. That is for why God created junior officers."

That wasn't what she'd been paid to find out. So Pantera toyed with his sated shaft as she pressed her luck a little harder, saying, "That dispatch still must have been most important, judging from the expression on your face when you read it, Querido."

He muttered, "It was. I don't know what poor Guatemala ever did to deserve so many enemies. That damned volcanic eruption up near the border has upset an already-delicate balance of power, and all sorts of people seem to feel this would be a very good time to readjust some disputed borders, damn their eyes!"

"That irregular column you sent out this evening should make short work of that Mexican land grab, no?" she asked.

He didn't answer. He was snoring softly. Pantera grimaced in disgust and gently disengaged herself from his limp and flabby old arm, saying quietly, "I must go to make poo-poo, you wicked fucker."

He didn't seem to hear or care. So the naked spy slid off the bed to dress swiftly, watching her exhausted, sleeping victim's slack-jawed face for any flicker of interest. When she had her clothes back on, save for her shoes, she smiled down at him with cold contempt and said to herself, "It's so easy to knock them out with a few little ass wiggles."

Then she moved across the soft rug, barefoot, to help herself to the dispatches in the breast pocket of the general's tunic, draped over a chair near the door. She didn't take time to read them. She didn't really care that much about their contents. She knew the people she was working for would pay her well for this night's work. So *they* could worry about what the Guatemalan junta might or might not be planning to do about the other invasion force from the northeast.

She turned for one last look at the old man sprawled across the bed and blew him a mocking kiss. It had been like taking candy from a baby. She turned away, gingerly and silently slid the bolt of the old man's bedroom door, and started to step out into the dark corridor.

She didn't make it. Pantera never knew what hit her as the general's .45 roared thrice, filling the room with gun smoke, and Pantera's back with hot lead! The black-clad spy was dead before she hit the corridor tiles with her face, smashing her nose, but one bare foot twitched like the tail of a stomped snake. So as the general rolled out of bed, gun in hand, he put a couple more rounds into her for luck.

He'd just put his teeth back in and was groping for his pants when a worried officer of the day came up the corridor, his own gun in hand, to stop and stare wordlessly at the general through the doorway, with Pantera oozing crimson on the floor between them.

The general sat on the bed and placed his still-smoking gun on the sheets beside him as he calmly hauled on his pants, saying, "She thought I was as dumb as I looked. Too bad. She was a fantastic lay. Is Major Rosas on the post, Lieutenant?"

"No, My General. He said you had issued him a three-day pass when he left, an hour or so ago."

The general nodded and said, "I did. I thought I owed him a favor. But no matter. We can court-martial him when and if he returns. If he is more than simply stupid, he probably won't."

The OD looked down at the body at his feet and asked, "Is it permitted to ask for why this lady has been shot, My General? I must put something on the morning report, unless my general instructs me not to, of course."

The old man said, "Come in and help me on with my boots, Lieutenant. Of course you will put it in the morning report. I deserve another medal for catching a spy in the act."

The OD stepped gingerly over the female corpse and came

to join his superior by the bed as he asked respectfully, "Was she really a spy, Sir?"

"Pick up my fucking boots, you idiot. I'll get the socks. Do I look like the kind of man who'd shoot a woman just for saying no? I didn't think she was a spy, either, until she started asking questions I saw no reason for a mere camp follower to be interested in. A cheating wife taught me, long before you were born, the advantages of pretending to be asleep when a woman commences to behave in an unusual manner. I gave her the rope and she took it. I waited until she took some secret dispatches from my pocket before I hung her. Oh, by the way, you'd better roll her off them before she bleeds all over them. I'll put my own boots on."

The OD hurried back to the doorway to holster his revolver and drop to one knee beside Pantera's cadaver. He rolled the dead woman over and gasped as he said, "I know this puta, My General! The other junior officers called her Señorita Hairy Tits."

The general grumped on his boots and stood up, saying, "That does not surprise me. Perhaps Major Rosas was simply a fool, after all. She did have a very, ah, winning talent for making friends. What shape are those dispatches in, Lieutenant?"

The OD stood up again, holding the blood-soaked papers gingerly by one corner as he observed, "One of your bullets went through them, too, Sir."

The general grimaced and said, "Oh, well, that is for why they make us type everything in triplicate. I remember what they said, in any case. Toss them over there in my fireplace and I'll burn them when they're dry enough. We wouldn't want anyone to get hold of them, no matter how messy they are to read, eh?"

The OD crossed the room to drop the bloody papers atop the unlit kindling in the fireplace as the general stared absently at the curvaceous corpse just outside his door and muttered, half to himself, "I shouldn't have allowed myself to get so excited, but she was, in truth, a rather exciting woman. Now that I have all my wits about me again, I wish I'd been smart enough to take her alive. But the odds are ten to one she was working for the British, anyway."

The OD turned toward him, confused, and asked, "For why would the British be spying on us, My General? Forgive me, perhaps I am stupid, but I thought *Mexico* was invading us."

"They are," the general said grimly. "But El Presidente Diaz is not the only child molester seeking to take advantage of the chaos in Guatemala! You know, of course, that we have never recognized old Queen Victoria's claim to what she insists on calling British Honduras?"

The junior officer nodded, eager to please, and said, "Sí. Los Anglos seized the Guatemalan province of Belize while we were busy fighting the Spanish for our liberty. It says so in all our schoolbooks, my general!"

The general reached for his shirt as he smiled thinly and said, "Well, in truth the disputed territory was stolen from His Most Catholic Majesty by English buccaneers in the 1600s. But the point is that the land was stolen in the first place, and that Guatemala inherited all Spain's property in this part of the world."

The OD nodded and, like the good little Guatemalan schoolboy he'd once been, said firmly, "Sí, it is our patriotic duty for to drive los Anglos from our sacred soil."

The general said, "Let's not get carried away. We're talking about a lot of lowland swamp, and the damned British have already logged off most of the mahogany on their side of the disputed border by now. Our problem is that the greedy bastards want to move said border further west so they can cut some *more* mahogany! According to those dispatches the late Señorita Hairy Tits was so interested in, Queen Victoria is terribly worried about restoring law and order in our volcano-ravaged land, too. A regiment of Royal Marines has just started up the Rio Hondo in steam launches, escorted by a couple of British gunboats. Do I have to tell such an educated young man that the Hondo is navigable to well inside our borders even the damned British have agreed to, up until now?''

"No, My General. But Queen Victoria must be loco en la cabeza! Those earthquakes and volcanic eruptions did not take place anywhere near *that* part of our poor country! Our few Indio and gum-gathering citizens in that lowland area do not need for to be rescued by anyone.''

"The British seem to want to rescue them anyway. You are right about the country being mostly empty jungle. But, to the outside world, one part of Guatemala is much the same as any other, and, as everyone knows, once Queen Victoria's muchachos move in to protect somebody, they seem most reluctant to ever let them go.''

"But what about the Monroe Doctrine, My General?''

The general grimaced and said, "I've never read a full translation of it. Nobody in Washington ever asked anyone down here to sign it or even look at it. But it seems to be a rather flexible document where English-speaking cousins are concerned. No doubt the Yanqui, Cleveland, would frown if the British announced a simple land grab. But who can argue with a dear old lady who wishes only to save us adorable little brown children from a natural disaster, eh?''

The OD, who didn't feel particularly brown, frowned and asked, "Can we do nothing about such an outrage, My General?''

The older officer said, "Of course. That spy in the doorway was no doubt sent for to pump me for the details. We have naturally filed formal protests with both the British and American embassies, here in the capital, and with luck, the stupid Yanqui who's sleeping with a junta member's daughter may be persuaded to inform his government how crude this latest power play by the Widow of Windsor really is. Meanwhile, since we can't put anyone named Barrios or Cabrera in the field with enough troops to change his mission to a revolution, we are stuck with those unkempt but otherwise trustworthy soldiers of fortune, Captain Gringo and Gaston Verrier. They say he's tangled with Royal Marines before. So let us hope he can at least slow them down until Washington gets around to saying naughty-naughty to the sweet old hag they work for!''

"But, My General, you sent Captain Gringo *northwest,* for to fight *los federales,* no?''

"Don't tell me what I did or didn't do, God damn it! Naturally I mean to send a rider after him as soon as it stops raining. They won't have marched far, in this kind of weather. The Mexican problem can wait, for now. Diaz *is* in fact moving his so-called rescue operation into rough country broken up by ash falls and fresh lava flows. On top of that, los federales don't move on horseback as fast as those damned Royal Marines can march, and the bastards are in steam-driven power boats! At best, Diaz may grab a few square kilometers of ruined Guatemalan soil that won't be fit to cultivate for years, and, in any case, we can lick *him,* once we get to the bottom of this mysterious plot dividing the junta.''

The general finished buttoning his shirt, put on a Sam Browne, and began to reload his revolver before holstering it as he moved over to the doorway, nudged the dead woman with the toe of his boot, and said, ''You'd better get some of your enlisted guards for to dispose of this mess and mop the tiles. Make sure they don't blab about it. Let the people who sent her *guess* how well she made out.''

"Consider it done, My General. But may one ask where you want us to bury her remains?"

"It is not important, just so she vanishes without a trace. I shall be in the orderly room if you need me. I have to consider who I can spare for to reinforce Captain Gringo, now that our plans have to be changed. It would be suicide for him to hit Royal Marines with the forces I gave him for to just fight Mexicans.''

The rider sent after Captain Gringo's column in the morning never caught up with them. For one thing, the general had assumed that at sunrise the hard-driving soldier of fortune would still be a lot closer to Guatemala City than he was.

Captain Gringo had pushed his people and their mounts all night, despite the storm, allowing no more than a few moments' trail break once an hour to rest the mules. He'd told his men and their rain-soaked adelitas that people with their asses in comfy saddles didn't *need* any fucking rest so early in the game.

As Carmella had warned, and he'd expected, the sun rose to dry out a column that wasn't quite as long as he'd started out with. When he ordered a roll call during the first daylight trail break, it transpired that seventy-eight men and as many women had dropped out during the night march when their superiors hadn't been looking. But it could have been worse. All the deserters save for one junior officer and three non-coms had been buck-ass privates, and even the remaining adelitas seemed pleased when he congratulated them for showing that they were real men, after all.

They watered their mules at a mountain stream across the trail. It naturally took some time, and Gaston asked what time breakfast would be. Captain Gringo said, "Hold the thought. I want to pull a vanishing act before we break for grub."

He took an ordnance map from his saddlebag and unfolded it to read as his mule lowered its head to drink. He found the stream they'd stopped for and followed it west with his eyes on both the map and the real ground. Then he nodded, folded the map to put away, and told Gaston, "If we follow this creek uphill a few miles, there's a valley running more or less in line with this well-traveled trail. I want to get us the hell off it before we meet any travelers with big yaps."

Gaston stared soberly upstream and observed, "Merde alors, you are talking about white water running over slippery boulders, Dick."

"Yeah; that's why nobody will notice any hoofprints leaving the regular trail. Naturally we'll have to dismount and lead the mules on foot."

"Naturally, I adore wading up to my crotch over slippery boulders in ice-cold mountain water! Can't we at least wait until it warms up a bit? I am still très goose bumped in this clammy wet uniform, you Spartan maniac!"

Captain Gringo laughed and said, "The water will still be cold no matter how long we wait, and we've waited too long already. Don't worry. By noon it'll be so hot up there among the rimrocks you'll be wishing you were sitting on a block of ice."

"Sacre God damn, my poor blue balls won't thaw out for at least a week. You do intend to stop *somewhere* between here and the border, don't you?"

"Sure, we'll break for siesta once it's too hot to ride any

further. There may be some shade up in the hills. For the mules, I mean. Us little guys can always toss a shelter half over a couple of bushes for a shady rest. But we have to keep our mules in shape.''

''I'm so pleased to learn you worry about somebody in this très fatigué expedition, Dick. Why are you still pushing them so hard? We got rid of the crybabies last night, non?''

''We'll see, once we push what's left a little harder. I don't want any weaklings coming with us all the way, and, hell, last night was hardly a real initiation. Some of the guys still with us could have been *real* sissies, without the balls to desert, see?''

Gaston started to bitch some more about his own frozen balls, but Captain Gringo pulled his mount's head up and rode to gather his other leaders for a tactical discussion, explaining the change in route and telling those few who objected to just shut up and do as they were told.

And so, long before the general's dispatches ordering an even more abrupt change in route could reach him, Captain Gringo had led his people upstream beyond human ken.

The higher, rougher, intermountain trail, if one could call it that, allowed them to ride most of the time, even though it called for leading the protesting mules on foot over some of the rougher stretches. The crooked valley between boulder-covered ridges was choked in places by other boulders that recurring earthquakes had rolled down the dusty slopes on either side. The once-wooded valley also offered lots of rotting tree stumps to avoid.

Well before they passed the remains of a long-dead charcoal oven, it was obvious that the ubiquitous Guatemalan carboneros had gutted and abandoned this ruined landscape, and, since it couldn't be good for anything else now, Captain Gringo congratulated himself on choosing a route that a regiment could march by broad daylight, unobserved by anything more important than a circling buzzard or two.

The broad daylight of course started getting hot as hell well before noon. So when they found themselves in a narrow gut, shaded along one side by the still-slanting sun, he called a halt and told his people to make sure they watered and rubbed down their mules before they broke out the tobacco and grub.

He tied his own jaded mount to a clump of brush with a nose bag of parched corn after he'd watered it and dried its hide with gunny sacking. Then, since it would take some time for the adelitas to root out some firewood and do anything important with it, Captain Gringo took himself and a pair of field glasses up the slope for a look-see.

He made it topside and moved along the razorback ridge to where it peaked in a jumble of weathered gray boulders against the now-clear sky. He climbed up into a natural grass-lined crow's nest cradled by the bedrock and swept the horizon all around with his field glasses. They were farther from the regular trail than he'd imagined. But he was just as glad when he spotted an antlike rider down there to his east, under a cloud of dust that spelled a full gallop. He wondered idly what the guy was in such a hurry for. But it wasn't his problem. His problem was to get his column to the battle area without the whole world yelling about it. He knew that los federales had maps as well as spies, so his only chance of surprise lay in moving his people sneakily, well ahead of contact.

Far to the northwest, a dirty mushroom cloud of volcanic ash slanted southwest with the trade winds. He didn't think it could be his old pal, Boca Bruja. *That* volcano had to be farther north. He consulted his map and it told him the most likely new culprit would be a cone called Mount Santa Maria, near the town of Quezaltenango. No problem. Both the

volcano and the town it menaced were on the western slope of
the continental divide. El Presidente Diaz was building his
new railroad east of the divide, through otherwise deserted as
well as devastated country.

He dismissed all the scenery more than a few hours' march
away and studied the terrain his column would be moving
through once the sun got a bit more reasonable. The fold in
the upthrust sierra they'd been following so far seemed to
open up ahead, and, though he saw neither settled country nor
even distant chimney smoke ahead, it was only a question of
time, he knew. The land-hungry campesinos didn't allow
much ground flat enough to grow a corn stalk on to go to
waste, and any hillsides with enough grass to matter would be
grazed by some damned somebody, if only a goatherd. He
didn't want to meet a goatherd or anyone else before he lost
his column from enemy eyes in the rugged country he'd
chosen to advance through.

There were a couple of gaps in the ridge to the west, far
ahead. With luck, they'd be able to work even higher into the
hills, since the sierra had a more or less northwest-to-southeast
grain.

He went back down and found that his adelitas had tossed a
couple of tarps over bushes for shade. It was too hot to do
anything more interesting with the girls than eat and catch an
hour or so of sack time.

By high noon the brutal tropic sun had turned the valley to
a bake oven. The mules had no shade at all, and, had they
been horses, some might not have made it. But by 2:00 P.M.
the sun had moved far enough west to sort of shade at least
one wall of the valley. So he crawled out of his improvised
sunscreen and yelled that it was time to saddle up and ride
again.

A delegation of junior officers joined him as he was

saddling his own mule. Their preappointed spokesman said, "We are accustomed for to siesta until three or four, Yanqui."

Captain Gringo said, "Tough shit; and you'd better call me Captain Gringo if you don't want to use my brevet rank."

He nodded at another, whose name he knew, and added, "From here on we'd better have scouts out on point, Lieutenant Delgado. Your troop just volunteered for point position this afternoon. Pick a couple of your best riders to scout ahead. Getaway scout to stay within sight of the column and . . . Shit, you know how it's done."

Delgado frowned and said, "Sí, I know how it is done indeed, and you don't know what you are talking about, Gringo!"

The big Yank decked him with a left cross. As Delgado landed on his ass in the dust, Captain Gringo stepped clear of the others and snapped, "The rest of you stay out of this if you want to keep it fist city!"

Nobody else said anything as they each moved back a few wary paces. Captain Gringo nodded curtly, and as Delgado rose to one knee, looking more surprised than hurt, the American asked conversationally, "How do you want to end this, Delgado? You've got your gun. You've got your fists. Or we can shake and forget it. It's all the same to me."

Delgado protested, "Officers and gentlemen do not fight with their fists like peones!"

"Thanks for calling me a gentleman. You've still got a .45 on your hip, unless you're willing to shake hands and start soldiering!"

"I do not wish for to be your friend. You just struck me. But it is against regulations for to shoot a superior officer."

"Okay, now that you've called me a gentleman and your superior officer, you can get up and put your hands in your fucking pockets for all I care. Are the rest of you guys paying any attention at all to this conversation?''

There was a sullen murmur from the others all around, and Captain Gringo said, ''Bueno. Listen tight, because I don't like to repeat myself. We're nowhere near the enemy yet. So if any of you muchachos want to settle who's in command, fist-city style, here and now, I'll be a good sport about it. But get it out of your systems today or forever hold your peace. Because from this trail break forward, I'll expect you all to soldier, and anyone who disputes an order from me will be well advised to slap leather as he does so. I intend to kill him or die trying.''

He let that sink in before he added mildly, ''Delgado and I seem to have settled our minor differences of opinion. Does anyone else here want to slap leather or put up his dukes? Bueno. Get your people saddled up and let's get the fuck out of here!''

They moved off to do as they were told. Captain Gringo finished cinching up his own mule but didn't mount just yet. He patted its hot muzzle and soothed, ''I know, amigo. It's a cruel world, ain't it?''

Gaston came over to join them, leading his own mount. The Frenchman said, ''I was regarding your disciplinary problem at a discreet distance. It was très amusing.''

Captain Gringo nodded and said, ''I noticed. Thanks for covering me.''

''It was the least I could do, my boisterous child. Do you think it is over?''

''Quién sabe? Delgado must not have liked me all that much in the first place. From past experience I expect him to either start brownnosing me or to try and put a bullet in my back. I'd better keep him out on point until we see how well he can take a punch. Are your own cannoneers set to move out?"

"Oui. They'd no doubt move faster if we did not have to pack the useless field guns. What if we just kept the gunpowder and left the scrap iron behind, Dick? You know as well as I we'll never use the toy cannons."

"You'd better hang on to 'em anyway. For one thing, you can't afford to have them taken out of your pay, once this show is over."

"Merde alors, getting back alive is what I had in mind! How fast can a man run with a ton of useless dead weight? You know, of course, that once we hit los federales, some running indeed may be called for?"

"Jesus H. Christ, Gaston. Can't you wait until we're within a hundred miles of a whorehouse before you start worrying about catching the clap? We'd better mount up. I see most of the others have, and I must say, for a guy who just got a dusty ass, old Delgado's moving his troop out pretty sharp."

The two soldiers of fortune swung up into their saddles but stayed put for the moment as they let the column reform. Then Captain Gringo heeled his mule forward to fall in behind Delgado's last riders but ahead of everyone else. Martinez loped in to join them, calling out, "Some of my heavy-weapons men are having trouble getting ready back there, Captain Gringo. We were not expecting to leave so early and . . ."

"Ride back and tell them to get the lead out," Captain Gringo cut in, adding, "Have them catch up and pass the adelitas wherever the trail widens enough. I want those machine guns in the center of the column. What are you waiting for?"

Matinez saluted and wheeled his mule to ride back and

build a fire under his slowpokes. Gaston chuckled and said, "I know what distracted their attention to duty. It was too hot for me to play house with my *own* adelitas under a bush just now. By the way, that's *another* worry on my mind, Dick."

Captain Gringo nodded grimly and said, "Agreed. We've led more than one guerrilla band more sensible about their sex lives. But the big brass told me we had to haul all that pussy along, and at least they're mounted and armed. Have you been drilling your own two adelitas with their carbines, Gaston?"

"Merde alors, it's the *other* drilling they expect from a man my age that I am beginning to find très fatigué! You know the two mestizas assigned to me, of course?"

"Not in the biblical sense, but I've seen 'em around the campus and they're not bad. What about 'em?"

"I think Muhammad must have been a younger man than I am now when he wrote his Koran. He said a man should be satisfied with four women. He may have overstated the case. I think two would be just about right if one was, say, a petite brunette with big tits and the other was a big flat-chested blonde, or vice versa, hein?"

Captain Gringo chuckled and said, "I guess a little flat-chested brunette and a big chesty blonde would be as much fun. But you've *got* two dames. So what's your problem?"

"Lack of variety. One has a little more Indian blood than the other and they swear they are not related, but they may as well be twins, in the dark. As one leaps from the frying pan into the fire it feels as if he just grabbed the same one by mistake. They are both, as you say, très attractive, and they are both most enjoyable in bed. But, merde alors, it is like sleeping with one inflamed nymphomaniac, and my back is starting to give out! I, ah, don't suppose you would be willing to take one of them off my hands, hein? You can take your pick, and I can assure you they are both great lays, Dick!''

Captain Gringo shook his head and said, ''I already have one mestiza and my own back ain't what it used to be. You're right about the Koran overstating the needs of a guy with anything else to do. Four adelitas would be more than I could handle. The three I have are a bit much. Could I interest you in a redhead or a mulatto? Whichever you left me would be all the contrast I needed with the mestiza in the middle.''

Gaston grimaced and said, ''I know some night when I am stuck in a lonely bedroll with nobody but my fist for company I'll regret this. But no, thank you. A man my age must be sensible.''

Martinez rejoined them to report that the heavy weapons were bringing up the rear of the cavalry troop just behind them. So they stopped talking dirty before Martinez could ask if they wanted to swap dames with him. They both knew that the junior officer's own adelita, riding back with the others, was a sort of bitchy little Creole spitfire. It was his problem and they didn't want to hear about it.

As Captain Gringo had foreseen, the trail got a little cooler even as it got wider to the north. He turned in the saddle to look back and up. The slow trot they were moving at was kicking up more dust than he approved of. So he told Martinez to lope forward and tell the point to slow down until they made it through this powdery-dry stretch. As Martinez rode forward, Gaston asked, ''Who are we worried about this far south, Dick?''

Captain Gringo shrugged and said, ''Anyone who might wonder about a dust cloud hanging above the rimrocks between them and us. We'll make up the lost time after dark.''

"Sacre God damn, you mean to continue this nonsense all through the night, as well?"

"Not *all* through the night. Just most of it. The moon rises twenty minutes later every night. So that means when we stop at sunset we'll get to rest and grub ourselves and the mules a good two hours. Then we'll take advantage of the moonlight and cooler riding to eat all the dust and miles we can before the damned moon goes down on us again. I figure our morning break should last, oh, hell, let's be big about it and let 'em take four hours, right?"

"Your generosity underwhelms me. The catnaps might be enough, if we didn't have the women along. But boys will be boys, so you are really talking about perhaps an hour's sleep this evening and two or three in the morning, non?"

"If a guy's got enough energy to fuck, after riding all day, he doesn't need any sleep in the first place. It wasn't my idea to drag a regiment of snatch along."

"Oh, well, it takes almost as much time to masturbate, in any case. But you are going to end up with a très fatigué military organization by the time we meet the enemy, Dick!"

Captain Gringo shrugged and muttered, "War is a tedious trade," as he looked back again to see how they were doing with the dust.

They were doing better. The long column of mules was still raising one hell of a haze of dust as it plodded over bare powdered laterite. But now most of it was settling on everyone's sweaty head and shoulders instead of rising high above to give away their movement northwest.

Captain Gringo was of course only practicing common professional caution and had no idea whether anyone important was scanning the horizon with field glasses this far south of the disputed border. But his professionalism was already paying off as, off to his northeast at a lower elevation, one of the dispatch riders sent after them by GHQ rode into a small isolated army outpost just off the main trail.

The rider and his cavalry horse were covered with sweat and dust as he reined in and dismounted by the watering trough just inside the gate. A quartet of more-comfortable-looking men wearing the same Guatemalan uniforms watched, bemused, as the rider took off his kepi, filled it with water while his thirsty horse drank, and poured it over himself with a sigh of pure pleasure, saying, "Madre de Dios, that feels good!"

One of the men manning the post, wearing sergeant's stripes, came over to join him, agreeing that it was as hot as a whore's pillow on Saturday night before he asked, "What brings you here at such a horse-killing pace, corporal?"

The dispatch rider said, "I carry dispatches for that irregular column that must have passed you by now. I don't know how in God's name they've been moving so fast."

The sergeant smiled uncertainly and said, "Irregular column? We have seen no irregular column, Corporal. You are the first person in this man's army's uniform we have seen since sunrise. Nobody but a few civilians and of course the mail stage has been by here, going either way, up to now."

The dispatch rider swore and said, "Jesus, Maria, y José! Where in the name of El Diablo could that crazy Captain Gringo be? I know I never passed them on the post road. You say they have not made it this far from the city. What on earth is left?"

The sergeant shrugged and said, "Perhaps they took another road? Who is this Captain Gringo you speak of?"

"Oh, that's right, you wouldn't know. The big brass has sent a regimental combat team out under a Yanqui soldado de fortuna for to fight the cocksucking Mexicans. But his orders have been changed and I have new ones for him in my saddlebags. Do you have a *telegrafo* here?''

''Of course. For why did you think they left us out here in the middle of nowhere, for to guard the ants? As you can see, if you wish for to look up, the wires running north and south or east and west cross here. Who do you want to send a message to, *amigo*?''

''I must wire GHQ that I have lost the column. I was told not to come back until I delivered their new orders. But this is ridiculous. Perhaps one of the other riders has already caught up with them and they are already heading northeast.''

The sergeant nodded and said, ''That sounds logical. Come on inside and you can cool off with a *cerveza* while we send your wire, eh?''

The dispatch rider thought that was a hell of a good suggestion. So he went into the adobe post with the sergeant, but he never got his beer. The Mexican wearing the uniform of a Guatemalan noncom shot him, just inside the door, and called out to his comrades in the dooryard, ''One of you bring those dispatches in here *poco tiempo*!''

Then he stepped over the body just inside the doorway and moved to the telegraph set up across the room. The adobe walls were bullet-pocked and one of the glass batteries had been smashed in the fight for the outpost that morning, but the telegraph still worked.

One of the other spies brought the dispatches in to him as the fake sergeant sat at the telegraph table. He spread them by the sending key to read. Then he laughed and told his comrades, ''This is rich! The damned *British* are grabbing some land, too!''

''Is that allowed?'' asked the man who'd handed him the dispatches, adding, ''El Presidente will not like it if los Anglos muscle in on us, no?''

The head spy shook his head and said, "No problem. Queen Victoria wants a different slice of the pie. Guatemala is too big, anyway. Los Anglos can have the swamps to the northeast as long as they don't argue about our claim to the highland cattle country. I'd better put this on the wire north, before the stupid Guatemalans get wise to us. Our own general will be most pleased to learn he no longer has to worry about that maniac Captain Gringo. Nothing *else* they have this side of the border is anything to worry about."

"Sí, the ones manning this post fought like children. But who is this Captain Gringo I keep hearing so much about, Lieutenant? Why should one man worry our leaders so?"

The man at the telegraph set said, "Captain Gringo is not a man. He is a disaster looking for a place to happen. I traded shots with him one time, up near Mazatlán, and our general knows him all too well, too. That is for why we were sent down here for to find out which way he was coming. Thank God he seems, this time, to be a disaster the Royal Marines will have to deal with, the poor bastards!"

He started sending, in code of course, and made his message short and to the point. As he stopped, the key began to talk back to him, and he took down the first few words before he laughed and said, "Guatemala City is asking what on earth I just put on the wire. I think it's about time we got out of here, muchachos."

He rose and led the way outside and around to the back where their own horses and some other followers dressed in peon costume were waiting. He called up to his lookout on the roof, "Come on down, Chayo! We're pulling out!"

One of his men, wearing a Guatemalan uniform robbed from the dead, asked, "Should we not get out of these clothes, Lieutenant?" The man in command said, "Not yet. The bullet holes don't show, and what's a little dry blood among friends? You just saw how useful it was to be in enemy uniform while discussing battle plans with ill-trained pobrecitos.''

"But, Lieutenant, if we are caught in these uniforms they will shoot us, no?''

"Naturally. They will shoot us in any case, so let's not get caught.''

As the lookout dropped down to join them, the head spy asked, "See anything interesting up there, Chayo?''

The lookout, dressed as a Guatemalan private, shook his head as he patted the field-glass case against his chest and said, "No, my Lieutenant. Not even the leaves of the trees are moving, as far as the eye can see.''

"Bueno. That rider was right about them marching on the British instead of us. Vamanos, muchachos, this silence is starting to get on my nerves.''

The next few days were hell and the nights were not much better as Captain Gringo threaded his column northwest through the mountains. More than once they were forced to swing wider than they wanted to avoid an isolated settlement or band of woodcutters. When some of his junior officers asked if it wouldn't be simpler just to shoot the pobrecitos, he told them just to shut up and do as they were told. It was a waste of time, he knew, to lecture the ruling class down here about the way they treated their peasants. They probably enjoyed the constant revolutions their attitude spawned, and, what the hell, he knew that the Mexican federales ahead were even bigger bastards.

One morning as they were breaking camp a lot closer to the Mexican border than they'd started, Martinez reported to

Captain Gringo that they were missing a troop of light cavalry. Captain Gringo asked if they were talking about that many desertions from various outfits or one no-kidding unit. Martinez said, "Lieutenant Delgado and all his men slipped away in the hours before dawn, along with their mules and their women, of course."

Captain Gringo grimaced and said, "Thank God they didn't leave their adelitas behind."

"Permiso to send a couple of loyal troops after the traitors? They could not have ridden far yet, Captain Gringo!"

"Permiso denied. Let GHQ court-martial Delgado. It's a small country and I'm sure your army has Delgado's mama on file."

"But, Captain Gringo, they took all their arms and ammunition with them!"

"So what? The guys and even gals we have left are still packing all the arms and ammo they were issued. Let the crybabies go. I don't want our real men wasting blood and bullets on people they weren't sent to fight."

Martinez hesitated and asked, "Permiso for to speak one's mind about, ah, our leader's unusual views on military discipline?"

"If you're talking about the way I've been driving this outfit, I know what you're thinking, Martinez, and you're thinking right. I have been hazing hell out of everyone. God knows you all needed it. When I was an underclassman at West Point, I thought the hazing they put us through was pretty chickenshit, too, and a lot of it was. One plebe in my cadet company hanged himself in the latrine one night after the upperclassmen had given him a rough day. A dozen others decided it just wasn't worth it for a shavetail's pay and ran home to *their* mamas. But the rest of us *took* it. And when they sent us out West to fight Indians, even meaner than upperclassmen, nobody ran home to mama when the going got rough.''

Martinez shrugged and said, ''I have heard of the unusual training methods of you English-speaking people. Forgive me, I mean no disrespect, but I fail to understand the way your minds work. You are kind to animals, generous to defeated enemies, and cruel as devils to your own side!''

Captain Gringo laughed and said, ''You Spanish-speakers are kinder to your friends and crueler to animals and prisoners of war, so I guess it evens out. But maybe the reason we and the Brits can afford to be nice to the guys we lick is that we lick more people. I mean no insult, either, but it's a fact of life that a buck-ass private in the U.S. Army is subjected to more training and discipline than you guys put even your officers' corps through.''

''Perhaps. I must say soldiering under you the past few days has more than made up for any hazing they neglected to put us through up to now!''

''Hell, Martinez, I'm not even *trying* to turn them into the kind of troopers I led against Apache, back in the States. But, with luck, we may hit los federales with better soldados than they were planning on meeting!''

So they saddled up and rode, trail breaking just often enough to keep from killing the mules and the hell with their riders. He gave his followers time to eat, sleep, or screw, but not all three. Even his own oversexed adelitas were too worn out now to argue about which one slept with him, and one night the little mestiza, Elena, deserted with some other boys and girls who'd had enough. He still had more of a harem than he had time for. But the redhead and the mulatto were so saddle sore by now that he suspected they were flipping coins behind his back to see who got to sleep alone, for God's sake.

But one morning, just as some of his remaining people

were about to send another delegation to protest that they couldn't go on without at least another hour's sleep, Captain Gringo called a strategy meeting and told his officers, "The map says we're somewhere on the border, if anyone knows where the border is, in these fucking sierras. This canyon is the best camp site we've hit so far. There's water and grazing for the mules. The sun won't be so bad down here, except at high noon. So I'm leaving Martinez here in command."

"Where are *you* going, Captain Gringo?" Martinez asked.

The big Yank said, "Scouting. That Mexican invasion force is somewhere to our east on the open flats over that way, if they're serious about that narrow-gauge railroad. I'm taking Gaston and a couple of good mules over the ridges for a look-see. I know the rest of you will be unhappy as hell to have a full day or more off. But maybe your adelitas at least could use a rest."

There was a round of pleased laughter from all save Gaston, who said, "Oh, merci beaucoup! More riding over hill and dale was just what my adorable old ass needed. Won't we need some troopers to pack the machine gun, Dick?"

"We're not taking any heavy weapons. I only want to find out where the fuckers are, not fight 'em."

"What if they want to fight us?"

"Your adorable old ass gets to ride like hell, of course. No two guys are about to stop a whole army column, with or without a Maxim. Let's go. Martinez knows what to do *here*. So we'd better get over *there*."

A couple of hours later, the sun wasn't getting any cooler and Gaston was still bitching as the two soldiers of fortune rode alone through a narrow pass leading east. Captain

Gringo knew they still had a few more ridges to work their way over before they were likely to run into the main Mexican column. But if the commander on the other side had any brains at all, he'd have a few scouts of his own out in the high country on his right flank. So he told Gaston to shut up, adding, "Don't make it easy for the pricks. Let 'em sort of *guess* we're coming. Voices carry among these rocks, you know."

Gaston muttered, "Merde alors, you've gotten us hopelessly lost in this species of rock pile. There can't be another human soul for a day's ride!"

But he did shut up, at last, when Captain Gringo turned in the saddle and glared at him. It was well that he did so. For they'd only made it around some house-sized boulders half-blocking the pass when Captain Gringo heard the distant sad strumming of a Spanish guitar and reined in, muttering, "What the hell?"

"Must be a village ahead," Gaston said softly as they both dismounted and eased forward, leading their mules and holding their carbines in their free hands.

Captain Gringo murmured, "There's not supposed to *be* a village anywhere near here. This section on the map is blank. So not even this pass we found has been surveyed yet. I see another sierra ahead, and, yeah, we're talking about another secluded mountain valley nobody important knows about."

He stopped in the shade of another boulder to stare down into the flat grassy glen between the north–south ridges. The guitar music was coming from what looked from up here like a handful of ants gathered around a crumb. But a thin plume of blue woodsmoke rose from the crumb, so it had to be a campfire. He said, "I make it five riders enjoying a trail break. They've unloaded their pack mules and hobbled the brutes to graze all around. So they must not be planning on going anywhere too soon."

Gaston asked, "Federale patrol?"

Captain Gringo said, "No. Too many pack animals, and they're too relaxed, judging from the guitar concert. Listen, is that a *dame* singing?"

It was, they could tell, as they listened harder and a shift of the vagrant valley breeze carried the sweet sad sounds of an earthy contralto voice up to them. Captain Gringo observed, "Los federales march with adelitas, too, but not on scouting patrols. I make them smugglers or refugees from that Mexican advance. Let's go find out which."

Gaston started to object, but even he could see that no more than four in the mysterious party could be men, and both he and Captain Gringo were packing repeating carbines they knew how to use. So the two soldiers of fortune moved out in the open and down the slope, still leading their mules to keep anyone from mistaking them for hit-and-run raiders.

As the people around the fire spotted them, the guitar stopped as if someone had lifted a phonograph needle, and two of the figures stood up. The other three didn't, and Gaston said, "Eh bien, two men traveling with three women. They must have friends in these parts, unless they are simply idiots."

As they got within shouting range, one of the men by the fire called out, "That is far enough, Señores! Before we invite you to share our coffee and beans, we would like to know a little more about you, eh?"

Captain Gringo called back, "We are with the Guatemalan army and we seem to be lost. Have you seen any Mexican federales around here?"

"Not around *here,* God damn the milk of their mothers!

But the flats over to the east are crawling with the insects! You did say you were army men, not customs inspectors?"

Captain Gringo laughed and replied, "Our business is with an invading army, not honest men who perhaps do not have time to discuss their business in these mountains with fussy bureaucrats. We could, ah, make it worth your while if you would pinpoint the other side a little better for us, Señor."

"Come have some coffee with us and let us discuss it, eh?"

As the soldiers of fortune moved in, Captain Gringo murmured, "Watch my back and I'll watch yours, right?" and Gaston merely replied, "Merde alors!"

As they joined the party, one of the women suddenly gasped and jumped up, crying out, "Oh, it is Captain Gringo! Forget what you just said about the pistola under your serape, Tío Pedro! These are the hombres who saved mi madre, mi padre, y myself from the banditos that time!"

As the pretty little teen-ager ran over to wrap her arms around him, Captain Gringo kissed her forehead in a fatherly way and said, "I never expected to meet *you* here, Fabiola! What on earth are you doing down here in Guatemala?"

He knew the Mexican girl of old, albeit not as well as he'd have wanted, had there been time when they'd met up in Mexico on the run. She said, "Los rurales and federales have been scouring the sierras for peon men and women. They wish the men for to work on their new railroad. Do I have to tell you what they want the women for?"

"Not really. We knew they were utter bastards when we agreed to fight 'em for Guatemala. I, ah, see you and your friends brought all your household furnishings along as well, eh?"

Tío Pedro laughed, hunkering down to remove the coffee-pot from the fire as he said, "Since you are friends, after all,

I will tell you that before we ran from los federales we managed to pick up a few items of theirs for to pay us for the trouble of moving. Do your men need any nice new Krag rifles? We were hoping to meet some people here who might be in the market for repeating rifles.''

Fabiola led Captain Gringo to a seat by the fire and sat with one arm locked in his as she explained, ''I told you, that time up in Mexico, we smuggled arms to Caballero Blanco, the Guatemalan rebel leader.''

Captain Gringo shot Gaston across the fire a warning look. But the little Frenchman knew enough to keep his mouth shut when it was important.

Captain Gringo said, ''We have no need of rifles, Señor. But if you have .30-30 ammunition to sell, we may make a deal. It depends on whether I'll be leading my own people this way or not.''

He took out his survey map and spread it on the sand as he added, ''Would you be able to point out their present positions on this map?''

Tío Pedro stared blankly and said, ''Forgive me, I am not a well-educated man and I did not bring my reading glasses with me this trip. I do not use paper maps for to find my way through these hills. God gave me eyes for to see the rocks, the sun, the stars, but, when it comes to maps . . .''

Captain Gringo said he understood and put the map away as he tried, ''Could you guide us close enough to their positions for *me* to map them, then?''

Tío Pedro handed him a tin cup of coffee, saying, ''I could, but I will not, Señor. I am, as you see, an old man. May I tell you how I got to *be* such an old man? When I was just a muchacho, my wise old padre taught me never to go near los federales if I could possibly help it!''

''Is that how you got all those Mexican army rifles?''

"That was different. They came up into my canyons. When a man *has* to fight federales, he kills as many of the bastards as he can. But he does not go *looking* for a fight with los federales! Besides, my boys and me only jumped one lousy infantry company in our own hills. You are talking about a whole army of them to the east, with cavalry patrols and long-range artillery. You are welcome to look for them all you like, but not with *me* along!"

Little Fabiola said, "*I* will show you where they are, Deek." So both Captain Gringo and her uncle told her she was nuts, at once.

But Fabiola insisted, saying, "I know these hills better than any damned old federale, and I owe you my very life, Deek!"

He shook his head and said, "There's no sense saving a pretty girl's life unless she intends to go on living, Fabiola. You're just a kid. You don't know how serious this game is played."

"Do not mock a woman of the world!" she protested, adding, "I may be young, but I am not a silly virgin and I know every fold of these mountains as I know the palm of my hand! Tell him not to mock me, Tío Pedro!"

Her uncle sighed and said, "He is not mocking you, my child. He is stating the facts of life as they are. I see, now, he is as decent an hombre as you and my other kinsfolk who have met him say he is. In God's truth I would like to help your old friends if I could. But, to also state the facts of life as they are, I am afraid. I say this openly, with no shame. Were I younger and braver, I would guide Captain Gringo through the pass I think you mean, Fabiola. But I am old, and sensible enough to be afraid of death. She rides closer to me these days than she does to you. But just the same, I do not wish for to meet her."

Captain Gringo glanced at the only other man in the party. He was a little younger than Tío Pedro, but not much, and when Captain Gringo caught his eye, he looked down and murmured, "I am afraid, too."

The American nodded understandingly and asked if the pass they were talking about was safe to ride a mule through. Fabiola shook her curly brunette head and said, "No. It is little more than a cleft in a razorback sierra of black volcanic rock. That is for why I know I could lead you safely there and back, Deek. From the rimrocks we will have a wide view of the arid flats to the east. But to get at *us*, los federales would need *wings*! Even from this side, the way is most difficult a climb, on hands and knees in places."

Captain Gringo asked if she could at least point out the direction to him as he got to his feet, with her still clinging to him. She pointed to a buzzard wheeling high to the east and said, "If that bird were to lay an egg right . . . *there*, it would spatter pretty close to the cleft I speak of. There is no trail, of course. Once in a great while one of us smugglers might use the cleft for a lookout. No animals have any reason for to climb bare rocks to nowhere."

He nodded and said, "Gaston, I'll leave you here with our mules. It looks like about a mile of flats and a mile or more of uphill crawl. No sense both of us wearing holes in the knees of our pants, right?"

"That's the nicest thing you've said to me all day," said Gaston, sipping his coffee.

So Captain Gringo put his carbine back in its saddle boot and started legging off through the shin-deep, sun-killed grass to get it over with. He'd gone less than a quarter mile when Fabiola caught up with him, protesting that he walked too fast. He slowed a bit but kept walking, not wanting to lose the bearing he'd taken on the distant rimrocks as he said,

''Go back to the others, dammit. Didn't you hear a thing your uncle and me said?''

She said, ''Sí, but he is my uncle, not my father, and I am of age for to do as I wish. So I will lead you over the razorback, Deek.''

They were still arguing about it when the ground started sloping up ahead and he paused to get his bearings, muttering, ''Get out of here, you crazy kid. Let's see, I go this way, right?''

She laughed and said, ''Wrong. That opening is a shallow box canyon. We must trend more to the left.''

She took his arm again to steer him as he shrugged and said, ''Well, if you're sure they can't get up at us from the far side . . . But your uncle's not going to *like* this, Fabiola!''

''Pooh, what can a man who is afraid for to die do to a woman of spirit, eh?''

That made sense, sort of. Captain Gringo knew *he* couldn't spank her, either, and as she guided him up the rock-strewn slope he began to feel better about letting her tag along. He'd never have found the damned way on his own, he saw now.

As the slope got even steeper, Fabiola let go of his arm and moved ahead, bending from time to time to haul herself higher by grabbing a bush or bracing her hand on a big black boulder. It gave him a very interesting view up her peon skirt from time to time, as she wasn't wearing a thing under it. He'd forgotten what great legs the little mestiza had. Her bare ass wasn't bad, either.

He saw more and more of it as the going got tougher and they had literally to crawl like lizards over the jumbled black rock, with walls of the same hue rising steeply on either side, as she led him into the crack of the sierra while allowing him to see the fur-lined crack between her thighs so often that he suspected she was showing off. But he hadn't come all this way to come that way. So he told his tingling privates to behave themselves as he followed her higher and higher.

They came at last to a flat expanse of black sand between sheer slippery walls of black rock no wider than the hallway of a house. She straightened up and said, "Be careful, Deek. It drops off even steeper on the far side."

He moved past her gingerly and muttered, "That's for damned sure!" as he found himself above a gut-wrenching thousand-foot vertical drop. At least another thousand feet of less-steep talus sloping away from the base of the cliff put their observation post high enough above the flatter terrain to the east to see for miles, and Captain Gringo gasped when he saw what was down there.

Thanks to the recent volcanic eruptions this far north, the once-greener rolling plains below were covered with cigar-ash-gray volcanic dust as far as the eye could see. The Mexican army moving around down there like ants was stirring up a haze of the sterile choking dust as they worked more like beavers than ants.

Fabiola asked, "Are you pleased I led you up here, Deek?"

He said, "Querida, if I was any more pleased I'd take you home to mother! Can you tell which side of the border they're on, down there?"

"No. Neither Mexico nor Guatemala has ever agreed just where the line should run, and, as you see, it is all deserted dust flats anyway. For why would you wish to take me home to your mother, Deek?"

He got out his map and a stub pencil as he said, "Just a figure of speech. You wouldn't be able to talk to one another, anyway. Be quiet a moment, Querida. I've got to get all that down on this map. Jesus, this is better than having an observation balloon! If I was up in a balloon they'd spot me mapping their positions!"

He found a slab of fallen basalt near the edge and hunkered down to use it as a map table as he started sketching. He didn't bother with the cavalry screen out ahead of the main body. He knew they wouldn't be in the same place long enough to matter. But a cluster of pitched tents farther north didn't look like it was going anywhere soon, and, beyond it, the sunlight glinted on the twin ribbons of steel winding even farther north until it got lost in the horizon haze. He noted that some of the track workers wore peon white and straw sombreros. Tío Pedro had said they'd been drafting civilian labor, the lazy pricks.

Uniformed men on horseback rode up and down, trackside. You couldn't hear them, from up here, but he knew they were yelling threats and orders to move faster as the peones sweated in the killing sun to lay more ties and spike the rails to them. He spotted a distant plume of black smoke and noted on his map how they were running fresh supplies in from the north instead of stockpiling near the railhead. The work train came closer, winding more than he could understand, at first, until he realized that the flats down there were not as flat as they looked from this high and far away. He saw the work train rattle over a trestle built across a dry wash he hadn't even noticed until now. He grinned and penciled in the wash, noting that it had to be at least six to ten feet deep, if crossing it called for a bridge instead of fill. The train rolled into the advance camp and stopped. Workers hastened to dump loose ties and bundled rails off the flatcars as Captain Gringo muttered, "Sloppy. They should push the flatcars ahead and unhook them to send the locomotive back for more. But I guess engineers who have more slave labor than they know what to do with don't have to think ahead much."

He found a distant butte that was on his map and ran a more accurate survey, muttering, "Yeah, they're maybe five miles inside the Guatemalan border, according to Guatemala. So we don't have to be nice to 'em. Is there a better pass, maybe ten miles north of here, or hopefully less, where mounted troops could get through, Fabiola?''

She said she knew more than one, in an oddly husky voice. So he turned to look at her and saw she'd spread her skirt in the black sand and was reclining on it with a bored expression on her pretty face and not a stitch on her shapely young body. He blinked and asked, ''Why did you do that, Fabiola? It's not *that* hot up here.''

She answered calmly, ''You have called me Querida more than once. Were you mocking me again, Deek? It is not kind to mock a woman by calling her your sweetheart if you do not wish for to make love to her!''

He laughed. She looked hurt. So he said, ''You have, ah, matured a bit since last we met, haven't you? But I'm not finished mapping the enemy positions yet, Querida.''

She shrugged a naked shoulder and asked, ''Can't it wait? You are right about the way the trade wind blows through this narrow crevice, and I am getting a little chilled, alone like this. Can't you see my goose bumps, Deek?''

He grinned, put the map on the sand, and piled his own clothing atop it before crawling over to join her, saying, ''Honey, your bumps are just the way I like 'em!''

But he was sure, as he entered her tiny welcoming body, that he would feel a little guilty about all this, once he had his sanity back. He knew she couldn't be more than sixteen, if that, and even though she'd propositioned him once before, up in Mexico at an even younger age, he was afraid some people might consider it child molesting, until she wrapped her little brown arms and legs around him and proceeded to show him that whatever he was laying, it certainly was no *child!*

They climaxed quickly together like old friends, even though he'd never had her all the way before. As they lay entwined in each other's arms, getting their breath back, Fabiola asked him clinically, "Would you say I fuck like a woman of the world, Deek?"

He moved teasingly inside her and replied, "That's a safe assumption. I see you've had some practice since the last time we met, and, come to think of it, it wasn't that long ago!"

She said, "Sí; I told you, once a virgin has been raped there is little point in acting shy. For why did you refuse me after saving me from those banditos who mistreated me, Deek?"

"I dunno. Idealism, I suppose. Obviously you got more than one other older guy to show you how it was done, friendlier, right?"

"Sí. I love for to fuck, now that I have discovered how good it feels. But I am still a little cross with you, Deek. You refused for to teach me all about romance, after I asked you to, so politely."

"Don't you consider this a proper apology, Fabiola?" he asked, moving a bit faster as he began to wonder why he'd stopped.

She giggled and moved her tiny hips delightfully under him. But then she said, "Wait. Everybody does it this way. But one can see you are a man of experience and I wish for to know all the ways."

"Querida, there aren't all that many ways, and, with something as yummy as you, this way's just great!"

She said, "Sí, it feels muy bonito this way. But you are special to me, Deek. You saved mi madre, mi padre, y myself that time and I love you a little, I think."

"Don't talk dirty, kid."

"Oh, I do not really wish for to meet your madre, Deek. I

do not think I shall want to settle down with one man in particular until I am a little older. But you are still special, so I wish for to *remember* you as special, eh?''

He started moving in her faster. She sighed and murmured, ''Oh, que hermoso! That feels marvelous. But I have thought of you often since last we met, and I have wished often I could have given my virginity to you, Deek!''

He kissed her collarbone and murmured, ''Sounds like fun, but you'd been, ah, sort of gang-raped before we ever met.''

She sighed and said, ''Sí, I lost my maidenhead most uncomfortably. But I have yet to be ravaged in every manner, you know. No man but you has ever had me in my anus, querido mio!''

He laughed incredulously and said, ''No man *including* me, you mean! You don't know what you're talking about, Fabiola. I ought to be horsewhipped for abusing a child like you *this* way!''

''Pooh, lots of men have come in me, there. Won't you be a good sport and show me how it feels to be entered for the first time by a good friend?''

''I'm afraid of hurting you, Fabiola. Not many women like it that way, you know.''

''But I *don't* know, Deek. How am I to know what it feels like if you refuse to be nice to me?''

He laughed and said, ''Okay, you'll see. I doubt if I can even do it back there with such a little dame. But we can try. When it starts to hurt, just say so and we'll do it right some more.''

She didn't say it hurt, although she hissed and bit her lower lip when, after a little fumbling, he got the love-slicked head inside her rosebud anal opening. He asked, ''Is that enough to prove my point?''

"No!" she said. "I want it *all* in me that way!" So he gingerly moved in deeper and deeper until she clamped down on its roots with her anal muscles and gasped as she said, "Oh, that *does* feel like I am giving you my virginity, Deek!"

He said he guessed she was, in a way, and suggested they quit while they were ahead. But she sobbed and said, "No, not until you come in me there!" And so, since he sure as hell had to take it out or move it in something so hot and tight, he gently started to obey her odd request, as she moved her legs higher, begging for him to pound her harder and rob her of her remaining virginity. By the time he was able to let himself go enough to come in her, that way, Fabiola had started to play with her clit and empty front entrance. So he didn't ask her what she was getting out of it and he knew, wryly, that from the way she enjoyed it, he was certainly unlikely to be the last man she would ever play this coy trick on.

They walked hand in hand back to the smugglers' camp, with Fabiola looking sort of Mona Lisa when they rejoined the others and Gaston asked if they'd had any luck. Captain Gringo said, "Yeah, better luck than we deserved. I've got the Mexican invasion mapped pretty good, and the situation's better than I even hoped. The suckers don't act like they're expecting trouble this far north."

Gaston shrugged and said, "They wouldn't be expecting trouble *anywhere* if we were not a pair of idiots. How many troops are we talking about, Dick?"

"No more than a brigade, out on point. I guess they figure

on bringing in the main force once they have the tracks laid far enough south to matter.''

Gaston lit a smoke, shook his head wearily, and growled, ''Did you hear him, le bon Dieu? Only a brigade, the child says. We have less than a regiment now to attack a half a division, and he says it is better than he hoped, merde alors!''

Captain Gringo said, ''They're not expecting to be attacked by anything, from the way they're bunched up around the railhead with a few cavalry guys loping around in the middle distance for reasons that escaped me. Maybe they're afraid of getting lost. Meanwhile, Fabiola here was good enough to show me a couple of other passes to the north on the map.''

''Naturally no Mexican officer would be bright enough to have them guarded, hein?''

Fabiola said, ''I shall be most happy to guide you all through the ridge, Deek.''

But he said, ''No. This time I really mean it. Gaston has a point, for once.''

He turned to Tío Pedro and said, ''We'll buy your .30-30 rounds, señor. An outfit can never have too many bullets. But then I want you people to move on south. It's likely to get very noisy around here before it gets any quieter, agreed?''

''We were supposed to wait here for Caballero Blanco, Captain Gringo.''

''Yeah. I'm sorry to have to tell you this, but Caballero Blanco was killed a few weeks ago, over to the northwest. We, ah, read about it in the papers.''

Tío Pedro laughed and said, ''I spit on their newspapers. They are *always* saying Caballero Blanco has been killed. But he keeps showing up alive anyway.''

Captain Gringo didn't think it polite to tell the obvious friends of the notorious Caballero Blanco he'd killed the son of a bitch personally, so he could only say, ''This time it looks like they really got him. He and his big white hat were last seen full of bullets and under a volcanic lava flow, see?''

"Bah, I see nothing but more government lies. Caballero Blanco is too tough for to kill. But maybe I had better sell you some bullets and move further into the mountains, if you mean to start a war with Mexico.''

Captain Gringo didn't have time to discuss who'd started the war. He took out his wallet, peeled off a few bills, and told the old man to just leave the ammo behind when he left, adding that he ought to move poco tiempo. Then he kissed Fabiola adiós, in a fatherly way, and the two soldiers of fortune rode off.

They hadn't ridden far when Gaston chuckled and asked, "How was that flirtatious Fabiola between her adorable little thighs, my old and smug?''

Captain Gringo raised an eyebrow and asked, "Have you been sniffing under ladies' skirts again, you old dog?''

Gaston shook his head and said, "Mais non, I did not have to. There is nothing in this world that looks more contented than a cow who's just been milked or a woman who's just enjoyed an orgasm. But wasn't she a little young for you, Dick?''

"If they're big enough they're old enough. Let's change the subject. What did you make of the old man's insistence that Cabellero Blanco could still be alive?''

Gaston shrugged and said, "Jesse James could still be alive, to hear some people tell it. Nobody likes to write a folk hero off.''

"Yeah, but those smugglers couldn't be wandering around blind on the off chance they'd run into somebody under a big white sombrero. We shot it out with Caballero Blanco and his gang almost a month ago and that's time enough for the grapevine as well as the newspapers to spread the word. Do you think it's possible the son of a bitch survived somehow?''

Gaston said, ''Mais non, Dick. One of the things I admire most about you is that when you swat flies they never fly again. I am sure the species of insect you buried under hot lava over by Boca Bruja will stay buried for the foreseeable future. But there is another way it might work. Do you remember the amusing California bandit, Joaquín Murrieta? He was quite a hero to the downtrodden Hispanic community during the California gold rush.''

''That was a little before my time. I hadn't been born yet.''

''I was a little young to associate with Mexican bandits in those days, too. But when I was your age I met a man the age I am now who was a member of the posse they say killed Joaquín Murrieta, Dick.''

''Good for him. Has this got anything at all to do with Caballero Blanco?''

''Oui; the old posse rider told me he did not think they got the right man. They did kill a Mexican who more or less fit the description. But the description was more or less indeed. For a time they had the preserved head of the man they killed floating in a big glass jar in San Francisco. So, more than one victim Joaquín Murrieta had robbed was able to say, with some heat, that they'd been robbed by *another* Joaquín Murrieta. The local Mexicans, of course, just laughed.''

''You mean the posse just killed some innocent Mexican for the reward?''

''Mais non; that would have been dishonest. The gentleman whose head ended in the jar was indeed riding with a bandit gang when the posse caught up with them at Tule Lake. They even recovered loot from more than one stage holdup. But even as they were shooting it out with one Joaquín Murrieta at Tule Lake, another Joaquín Murrieta was robbing yet another stage near Angel's Camp. This is not as impossible as it sounds when one considers what Joaquín Murrieta *means*. Murrieta is not a common Spanish name, you see."

Captain Gringo thought. Then he nodded and said, "Right. It translates freely as Sullen Jack. But naturally the guy wouldn't have used his right name."

"Naturally. So, like Molly Maguire, Joaquín Murrieta was a nom de plume, used by any number of California Mexicans displeased with their new Anglo neighbors, hein?"

Captain Gringo nodded and said, "That works. There's no natural law preventing anyone from riding a white horse under a big white sombrero and calling himself the white knight."

"Oui; the one we shot it out with over by Boca Bruja could have been only one of a *set*! Tío Pedro could have run his guns down here to *another* Caballero Blanco, non?"

"Maybe. But in that case, where *is* the son of a bitch? We haven't met a soul in these mountains except those smugglers."

"True. But on the other hand we have been taking some pains to avoid meeting anyone. You have insisted on choosing routes a wild goat would not take, left to its own devices. In this maze of jagged rock we could have missed meeting any number of wandering bands, non?"

"That was the general idea. But we've found the pricks we were sent to find. So let's get back to camp and make some battle plans."

Gaston's casual ruminations regarding bandit bands in the surrounding hills had been closer to the mark than he'd seriously considered. As the two soldiers of fortune were riding into their own canyon camp, a man dressed all in white rode his white Spanish barb into the Mexican railhead camp at the head of his less glamorous but numerous followers.

The Mexican brigadier in command of the project came out of the command tent to greet him, repressing a smile of contempt as the bandit leader dismounted and waved the cavalry pennant he'd picked up somewhere in his travels. The Mexican officer asked, "What have you there, Caballero Blanco?"

The Guatemalan all in white replied, "A battle trophy, General. My boys and me ambushed a whole troop of Guatemalan cavalry in the hills to the south this morning. The idiots were riding along a canyon with no scouts ahead or covering their flanks. It was like taking candy from a baby." He reached in the breast pocket of his white kid charro outfit and took out a bloodstained booklet, adding, "Here is a bank book of their troop commander, one Lieutenant Delgado."

The Mexican leader looked both pleased and concerned as he said, "Bueno. Let us go inside and cool off with some cerveza while we consider the matter. Tell your men to water their mounts and grab something to eat. But make sure they are ready to move out again soon."

Caballero Blanco turned to his segundo and said, "You heard the general, Gordo. I shall be here if you need me. But do not need me unless it is important."

He followed the brigadier into the command tent. It was still too hot but at least bearable under the canvas shade. The brigadier reached into an ice bucket and produced two bottles of beer brought in by train along with the ice a few hours before. The officer uncapped his bottle with a handy bottle opener. Caballero Blanco uncapped his with his teeth. The Mexican didn't comment. He was used to the breed. *This* uncouth bully at least seemed to be useful.

The brigadier waved the bandit to a folding canvas seat at the map table in the center of the command tent and took his own place across from Caballero Blanco. He took a swig of cerveza and asked, "Could you pinpoint where you encountered these unfortunate cavalry troopers on the map, Caballero Blanco?"

The bandit nodded and stabbed a dirty fingernail down on the chart paper, saying, "Sí; it was here, where this stream cuts out of the sierras to the lower plains. They were following the water."

"Were they riding north or south? It's important."

"They were riding south, General. For why is it important?"

The brigadier looked relieved and said, "It fits what our other intelligence reports said. Apparently the Guatemalans really feel we are less of a threat to them than the British expedition to the northeast. They are wrong, but that is *their* problem. The troop you jumped must have received the new orders too. What did you get out of the prisoners you captured?"

"Prisoners? For why would I take lousy prisoners, General?"

"Never mind. It was a foolish question. Did you encounter any *other* Guatemalan forces over in the hills to the west?"

Caballero Blanco shook his head and said, "If we had, we would have brought you their pennants, too. My boys and me swept all the usual smugglers' trails through the sierras, as you asked. The only people we encountered were, of course, some smugglers. I recognized them through my field glasses, so I did not see fit to attack old friends. But, knowing my Mexican comrades wished to keep this visit a secret, I did not contact them. Too bad. One of the women traveling with Tío Pedro had a most presentable little ass."

He took a healthy swig of cerveza, allowing some of it to run down his unshaven chin as the Mexican across the table suppressed a grimace of disgust. Then he belched and said, "I would like to talk to you about my devotion to your cause, General. I know you have promised me I will be the governor-general of the new Mexican estada of Nuevo Chiapas, once the territory has been taken. But, with all due respect, I have nothing in *writing* to this effect."

The brigadier frowned and asked, "Do you question the word of a Mexican officer and gentleman? Be careful how you *answer* that, Hombre!"

Caballero Blanco said, "I do not doubt your word for a minute, my Mexican liberator. But it would be easier to convince the local little people their bread is buttered on my side if I had some proof I would soon be governing them wisely and well for El Presidente Diaz. You see, forgive me, I love your presidente, myself, but some of our uneducated campesinos fail to grasp all the advantages of Mexican rule. For some reason, they seem to prefer the government they already have in Guatemala City. I keep assuring them the taxes will only go up a little, hardly enough to matter, but they keep asking how a Guatemalan like myself would be in a position to know. There is yet another problem my muchachos and me have, working for you without a thing on paper. Some of my men have been wondering what happens if they are captured by Guatemala while serving Mexico with neither uniforms nor documentation."

The brigadier shrugged and said, "That's easy to answer. I strongly advise you not to be captured. But what are you worried about? I just told you the weak and divided Guatemalan junta has sent the few field forces it can trust against the British, at least two hundred kilometers from here. As for your commission, you will get your damned commission when Mexico City *sends* your damned commission! *I* have no power to make Mexican officials of Guatemalan turncoats in the field."

"Hey, that is not a nice thing for to call a *friend*, General!"

The brigadier still needed the services of the unwashed lout. So he forced himself to smile as he asked soothingly, "Hey, can't you take a little kidding, hombre? I've wired the capital about your generous offer to help us liberate your part of Guatemala, and it's only a question of time before they send your papers down by train. They could be on the way right now, see? A special carrying troops and mail will arrive this very night."

"Bueno. I shall be most anxious to see if I get any mail."

The brigadier shook his head and said, "You won't be here. I have another mission for you and your muchachos. Now that you've patrolled the ranges to the west, I wish for you to patrol to the east, between us and those mysterious Royal Marines."

Caballero Blanco gasped and asked, "You are sending me for to fight Royal Marines, with a hundred riders and no heavy weapons?"

"Of course not. I just said the British are over two hundred kilometers away. Our agents report them somewhere on the Rio Hondo, in the lowland jungles. They know better than to grab more than the northeast panhandle of Guatemala if they do not wish our presidente to evoke the Monroe Doctrine with his Yanqui friends along the Street of Walls in Nuevo York. But between us and the British lies a no-man's-land of partly unmapped mystery. The Guatemalan forces sent to resist the British will be somewhere among the confusing drainage of the Rio Usumacinta's headwaters. It's made for guerrilla operations, and we know the Guatemalan junta has hired a notorious guerrilla leader to lead their counterattack. I wish to be certain the insane Yanqui known as Captain Gringo

is closer to the British than he is to *me!* So I am using you
and your band as a screen for my left flank, see?''

Caballero Blanco looked dubious and said, ''I have heard
of this Captain Gringo, too. They tell me he killed me one
time. If it is all the same to you, General, I'd rather fight
someone else!''

''Idioto, I don't expect you to fight with Captain Gringo
and the Guatemalan army he leads! I only want scouts, plenty
of scouts, out between my left flank and him. If you spot so
much as the trail dust of an army column on the move, you
will of course avoid any contact and dash back here at once
with the news. I have more big guns coming down tonight by
train. But I do not wish for to waste time setting them up to
cover my left flank unless I need to.'' He drained the last of
his bottle and added, ''I would, ah, like my left flank covered
as soon as possible, Caballero Blanco.''

So the traitor finished his own cerveza, belched again, and
went out to gather his men.

An aide came in to report, ''The enemy seems to have
gotten wise to our tapping into his telegraph lines, sir. The
line's been cut south of Chajul. But naturally we are still on
the wire to the north.''

The brigadier smiled thinly and said, ''Bueno. The line
would have been cut closer to this position if there were even
Guatemalan scouts within a two-day ride. But I will still feel
better once those extra troops and guns arrive tonight.''

The aide shrugged and said, ''We are in a good position
here for to take on anything they have up their sleeves, no?''

The brigadier said, ''I hope so. In any case, I have done all
I can for now. The hills on our right flank have been well
scouted and found empty. Our guerrillas are just riding out for
to cover our left flank, and it would be suicide for even
Captain Gringo to attack us across wide-open ground from

the south. I want our pickets out there half a kilometer after dark, anyway.''

"It shall be attended to, Sir. I just saw that puffed-up idiot in the white suit getting his patrol together. Are we really going to let him run this area, once we take it, Sir?''

"Don't be an idiot. The illiterate thug has his uses, at the moment. But naturally, as soon as we have no more use for him, he goes against the nearest wall with the other local Guatemalans of any importance.''

Late that same afternoon, Captain Gringo led his expedition as far as the now abandoned smugglers' camp and had them pick up the ammo Tío Pedro had left near his extinguished fire. The big Yank told his followers not to build any others, but that it was okay to let the mules graze for the moment, as long as they remained saddled. Then he went back up the slot Fabiola had shown him, this time alone, to make sure nothing important had happened since the last time he'd mapped the Mexican positions. Nothing had. The work gang had laid a few more yards of track. The mounted pickets had moved a little farther south. The battery of sandbagged field guns he'd noted earlier was still in place, covering the open ground Mexico was bent on invading.

When he rejoined his own column and gathered the officers and noncoms for an update, Gaston raised the question of their own field guns again, saying, "I see no reason for packing useless scrap iron along on a hit-and-run raid, Dick. As I understand your très risky plan, we hopefully won't stand still in any one place long enough for me to even mount my adorable little toys.''

Captain Gringo said, "Your pack mules are coming with us

anyway. So, what the hell. You never know when even a small-bore field piece might come in handy, Gaston.''

A junior officer suggested leaving the adelitas and other clumsy baggage in a base camp here during their attack. Captain Gringo thought that was even dumber, but was polite enough to explain, ''We won't be coming back this way, Ortega. That's what they'll be expecting us to do, once we hit 'em from the hills, and they *do* have field guns that can lob real stuff a good five miles or more. Like I said, we'll do all the damage we can and then withdraw to the east along that dry wash I spotted cutting across their rear.''

He glanced up at the sun before adding, ''Okay, we want to hit the gap in the rimrocks to our north just about sundown. Naturally I'll be scouting well ahead in case some wise-ass Mexicans have the pass on a better map. That still leaves us a couple of hours to relax and eat some cold grub. Tell your adelitas to whip up some tortilla-and-cold-canned-bean sandwiches for you. But go easy on enjoying any other delights they might have to offer. We can all get laid *after* the battle. I want us all in shape for some fancy broken field running tonight!''

There was an amused chuckle all around, and Captain Gringo decided it was time to boost the moral of his enlisted men, now that his officers and noncoms seemed to be learning to soldier.

He had Martinez form the dismounted troops into a close formation around him as he climbed up on a stack of ammo cases, yelled at them to all shut up and pay attention, then shouted, ''Hacer caso, prestar atención, you chattering urraca cabrónes! I still don't think the whole bunch of you would make a pimple on a real soldado's ass, but at least you've made it this far, which is more than some of the crybabies we started out with will ever be able to tell *their* grandchildren!

Your officers and noncoms have their orders. So all you stupid bastards have to know is that this is it. We're going into battle tonight, and I don't leave my wounded behind. So if you have to get your stupid selves shot, for God's sake be considerate enough to die so the rest of us won't have to carry you."

As he'd hoped, more of them laughed than cursed, and one called out, "Who gets to carry *your* big Yanqui ass, Captain Gringo?"

He joined in the laughter and then said, "If I get hit, I'll deserve it. I don't want any heroics. I want you to do just as your leaders tell you to and let the dumb Mexicans play hero. Anyone who ever told you it was your duty to die for your country was full of shit. It's your duty to make the enemy die for *his* country. Some of you will be worried about your adelitas. I may as well tell you that some of the chickenshit officers you love so much already asked me how we'll protect the mujeres. You have my word they'll be led to safety before the balloon goes up. You also have my word that any man who drops out of the firing line to see if his private pussy is all right will be shot for misbehavior before the enemy. Nobody, repeat nobody, is supposed to think for himself under fire unless or until everyone around him who outranks him has bought the farm."

A man in the rear ranks shouted, "What happens if even my squad leader falls in battle, Captain Gringo?"

"You run like hell if you don't have the balls to go on fighting. Just remember that any man who runs tonight had better keep running. Because if the Mexicans don't kill him when they catch him, I will! Are there any other questions?"

Another trooper raised his hand and called out, "Sí. I would like for to know, with no bullshit, just what our chances are of winning tonight!"

Captain Gringo shrugged and said, "Less than fifty–fifty. You'll be fighting way outnumbered and outgunned, and you know you're not worth shit as soldados. The only thing you have going for you is that the Mexicans may not be worth shit either."

There was a roar of protest and another man yelled, "By the beard of Christ, my old grandmother can lick any fucking Mexican!" and, from the roar of agreement all around, Captain Gringo knew they were ready.

No federales were posted to guard the pass Fabiola had told Captain Gringo about. The pass wasn't on the Mexican brigadier's map. So, before the moon rose, the Guatemalan column was moving east below the rim of the dry wash running behind the Mexican railhead. Naturally, every man and woman in Captain Gringo's command led his or her mule on foot, keeping a hand on its muzzle in case it chose such a dismal time to bray. But the mules by now were too well trail broken, or perhaps just too tired, to comment freely on their new surroundings. The wash was paved with soft sand, muffling the occasional stumble of foot or hoof. Captain Gringo halted his advance just out of rifle range from the trestle across the wash ahead and sent Gaston and a couple of likely lads to scout it. Gaston returned within minutes to report, "Eh bien, all clear. My boys are watching the tracks, both ways, and have orders to fire their carbines if a track patrol comes from either direction."

"Weren't there any guards at all posted on that trestle, Gaston?"

"There was one. He is no longer with us. Young Moresco

is almost as good as me when it comes to throwing knives in tricky light.''

Captain Gringo nodded and signaled the others to follow as he moved on. Some of the mules tried to bitch about it, going under the trestle with the smell of blood in the air. But the human hands clamping their nostrils prevented them from braying.

Captain Gringo stopped under the trestle and hissed Carmella over to take charge of his own mules as well as hers, saying, ''I want you and the other adelitas to dig in at least two kilometers to the east, Querida.''

''So far?'' the redhead protested, adding, ''We girls have guns, too, you know.''

''Yeah, and you may still get to use 'em. Get going, Carmella!''

She did. So it was Alicia's turn to stop and tell him how much she wanted to fight by his side, until he slapped her on the rump and sent her after his other adelita.

He spotted Martinez leading the heavy-weapons troop and quietly called out, ''This is as far as the machine guns go, Martinez. I want you to set up a hundred meters to the east with your own gun crew, facing south. Leave one of the Maxims and a couple of ammo cases here with me.''

''You intend to set up here, at this bridge?''

''Do I look crazy? I'll dump the water from the jacket, scrap the tripod, and sort of handle a roving assignment to the west. Gaston will be in command of everybody on your side of this trestle. Are you paying attention, Gaston?''

''Oui. I was about to suggest I'd feel much safer over that way in any case. What is the form if you manage to get cut off from us, Dick?''

''You get our people out the best way you can, of course. Los federales will be expecting a retreat back into the hills to the west. Hopefully I can convince 'em with scattered bursts of automatic fire. You know the plot of the first act. Use your own judgment on when it's time to drop the curtain and exit stage left. Where the hell is that gunpowder you've been bitching all this time about bringing along?''

Gaston said, ''It should be here shortly, avec those useless mountain guns. May I leave *them* in your care, too?''

''I told you to hang on to them, dammit. I just need a half-dozen kegs that go boomp in the night, for now.''

A gaggle of adelitas passed. Then he spotted the overloaded artillery mules and stopped them long enough to have Gaston's gunners drop off the powder kegs and fuse roll that his plan called for. A troop of light cavalry brought up the rear. Captain Gringo called out softly, ''Let's move it, Ortega! You know where you and your men form your fire line, I hope?''

The junior officer looked hurt as he replied, ''Sí; on Lieutenant Romero's left flank, between him and the adelitas.''

''Make sure you're the last to pull out, too. I want a steady drumfire from your troop as the others evacuate past you, remember?''

''Jesus, Maria, y José, how many times do you have to give a man the same orders, Captain Gringo?''

''Sometimes a hundred times is not enough. Get going, Amigo!''

That left nobody west of the trestle. Gaston asked, ''Do you need help setting up your ingenious ruse, my mischievous elf?''

Captain Gringo said, ''No, I need somebody in command to the fucking east. If I don't make it, just lead them east until you're sure you're out of contact with these pricks, and then swing south for home base.''

''Merde alors, Ortega was right, and you keep saying *I* talk too much. I know how to lead a fighting retreat. I was on more than one losing side before you were born. But...Dick?''

''Yeah?''

''Be careful, hein? This idea of yours is très wild, even for *you!*''

''Get going, you old basser.''

So Gaston moved out of sight down the wash as Captain Gringo got to work, feeling sort of lonely all of a sudden, for some reason.

He left the Maxim and machine-gun ammo under the trestle with the dead guard for the moment as he lugged two kegs of gunpowder south toward the distant pinpoints of light that gave away the position of the Mexican railhead encampment. Midway between them and the railroad trestle over the wash, he hunkered down and proceeded to bury one keg between two ties, scooping ballast out as quietly as he could with an otherwise useless leg of the machine-gun tripod. He'd just gotten it in place when he heard the crunch of leather on ballast and saw one of the camp lights wink out for a moment as someone passed in front of it.

He remained crouched between the rails, drawing a blade from his belt. The corporal of the guard never knew he was in trouble until too late. He walked into Captain Gringo's knife, still whistling ''La Paloma'' under his breath, and didn't make enough of a thud to matter when he fell dead across a rail.

Captain Gringo rolled him off to one side and went back to fusing his improvised land mine. Then he moved back to the second keg, unreeling fuse, and repeated the process. He left the coil where it was, went and got two more kegs, and in the end had a line of four fused at fifty-meter intervals between the rails.

The remaining charges were placed to blow up the trestle,

of course. He unreeled fuse west as far as it lasted, which left him closer to the trestle than he really wanted to be when he carried the stripped-down Maxim as far west as he could take it and, since he still seemed to have the time, proceeded to do other sneaky tricks with his machine-gun-ammo belts. They were the newest thing in webbing, as he'd noted before, so it was possible, albeit not recommended, to clip one belt to another. He did so. The end result was almost seventy-five feet of belting he wouldn't have to change, even if it did threaten to trip him up or jam the gun if he wasn't careful.

The moon was rising now. It was surprising, even to Captain Gringo, how peaceful and serene the dusty gray plain still looked by the light of the tropic moon. He could only hope the others were in place. If they were not, this was going to wind up a very messy flop.

The moon had been the signal they'd agreed upon beforehand, so he dropped below the rim of the wash and lit a now somewhat wilted Havana claro. He held it cupped in his hand as he eased up for a better view before lighting the fuse in his other hand.

He'd just done so when, behind him, he heard a mournful locomotive whistle and turned, cursing, to see the headlight of another train coming down out of the north!

He said, "I take that back!" as he groped for the fuse he'd just lit, grabbed it, and tried to pinch it out. But he couldn't tell for sure whether he had or not, and, damn it to hell, there went a great chance to blow a train as well as the trestle! The son of a bitch was coming too fast and was sure to cross the wash before the trestle blew!

A weak spot in the fuse coating, ten or more feet away, sputtered enough to give away the fact that the fuse was still lit and, okay, even burning fast it wasn't going to beat that fucking train to the crossing!

It didn't. He was out of range of the locomotive's beam along the track. So he didn't have to duck as it thundered safely over the trestle. He just got to call it terrible names as he saw it was another string of flats loaded with ties and rails. It sounded its whistle again as it slowed beyond the trestle, and, to the south, tent flaps opened to spill light as the Mexicans expecting it stepped out to greet it. Captain Gringo shrugged and muttered, "Oh, well, at least they won't be able to back out, this time."

He picked up the primed Maxim and lay prone above the rim of the wash as he waited for the bridge to blow. It seemed to be taking its time, damn that fuse. And then, as he waited, he heard yet another railroad whistle blow behind him, and when he turned his head, he saw *another* train coming!

He grinned and prayed, "Please, fuse, don't fuck up again on me!"

He knew, of course, that there was no way to time it exactly and that with any luck the second train would be on one side or the other when the trestle blew.

But not even El Presidente Diaz could be lucky every time, and so, just as the second locomotive made it across the trestle and Captain Gringo swore, the gunpowder he'd placed exploded with a roar directly under the troop train the locomotive was pulling!

The cars on the trestle went up and then came down ass-over-teakettle in a chaos of echoing explosion, smashing wood, and human screams!

As the wreckage piled up in the dry wash, oil lamps intended merely to illuminate the interior of the troop train for its military passengers set the shattered varnished wood afire to cremate the dead and burn anyone too badly hurt to crawl out alive. But as some few made it, outlined against the burning wreckage, Captain Gringo growled, "The hell you say!'' and opened up on them with machine-gun fire, to play this new development by ear.

From the sounds of gunfire on the far side of the flaming wreckage, more than one of his followers was a quick study, too!

Meanwhile, it got even worse for the invasion forces. The troop train's locomotive, having escaped the death trap at the trestle, just kept going fast as its bewildered crew jumped out of the cab to figure out, later, why they were still alive. So the troop-train locomotive barreled down the single narrow-gauge track to smash into the work train at full speed, folding up the flatcars like an accordion and pinwheeling ties and long lengths of steel rail into tents and human flesh all over the encampment before the combined new wreckage burst into flames.

But los federales, as Captain Gringo knew, were not sissies. So he wasn't really surprised to see a skirmish line outlined by firelight coming his way on either side and across the tracks. He did know he had a better view of them than they could have of him with nothing but darkness at his back. So he got to his feet, making sure the long ammo belt wasn't kinked, and started firing short bursts into them as he crabbed sideways toward the mountains.

On the far side of the burning wreckage in the wash, Martinez took that as his signal to open fire with his own machine gun, even before other Guatemalans to the east opened up with a withering, steady fusillade of carbine fire.

A Mexican officer blew a whistle and the skirmishers fell back. Then the charges Captain Gringo had placed between the tracks started going off one by one, as if heavy artillery shells were chasing them back to camp. So, though only one poor slob was unlucky enough to be blown high in the sky like a screaming rag doll, the others were running like hell by the time they were out of range, and they were the lucky ones. The skirmishers had left more men dead or dying on the ground than got away.

But as Captain Gringo and Gaston had learned more than once, the hard way, one could never kill enough federales. El Presidente Diaz got them cheap and their officers used them the way more-humane leaders used toilet paper. So the big Yank wasn't surprisded when another skirmish line formed up again, this one mounted, to try a little harder.

The American felt sorry for the Mexican horses as he and Martinez spilled rider after rider with their crossed machine-gun fire. And while he could hardly admire the manners of los federales, he had to admire the guts of more than one spilled rider who picked himself up and kept coming on foot.

But it took more than guts to carry a man through the withering fire of two Maxims and hundreds of blazing Guatemalan carbines. So the second charge failed, even bloodier, as the brave but badly commanded federales littered the open flats with their dead and dying.

Captain Gringo had warned his own people not to count on the third time being a charm. Hence, he knew Gaston would be moving the others out by now as Ortega's troop kept firing enough to keep it from becoming obvious.

In the distance, outlined by the flaming wreckage at the end of the rails, he saw other Mexicans forming to do something or other. He leaped to his feet and crabbed west toward the mountains, firing short bursts as he pretended to be a whole regiment retreating back into the hills. Ortega, as planned, had by now ceased fire and would be covering the rear as the others really retreated east.

Captain Gringo wasn't sure his ruse was working until the long dragging ammo belt snagged on a dead stump of chaparral, whiplashed around, and tripped him up. He fell, cursing, and rolled to keep from driving the muzzle of his Maxim into the gritty ash. Then a twelve-pound shell whizzed over him, waist high, to explode close enough to make his ears ring and make him very happy to be flat on the ground!

He dragged himself and the Maxim back over the edge of the dry wash and ran up it fast, as shell after shell exploded on the flats all around to add wings to his heels. Some few landed in the wash itself, albeit not close enough to nail him as the federales nibbled at his bait.

He got out of the barrage, braced the Maxim over the rim of the wash, and fired a hopelessly long-range but defiant burst.

It worked. He muttered, "Me and my big Maxim!" as he ran like hell in the other direction while the federales laid a walking barrage between his last known address and the mountains they thought he was making for.

His ammo now exhausted, Captain Gringo climbed out the far side of the wash and made tracks north across the dark deserted flats as the federales wasted a lot of expensive shells off to the west. The empty Maxim was hot as well as heavy and he knew he had some catching up to do indeed. He'd have to swing wide to the north before crossing the tracks. He was on foot. Gaston and the others were not only mounted but doubtless riding like hell for their lives before los federales could come unstuck. They'd done what they could to mess up the Mexican advance, and that railroad wasn't going anywhere for a while. But they hadn't killed nearly enough federales to have a chance with the superior arms and numbers left.

He was tempted to chuck the Maxim. It was empty. It had done its job. But there was more ammo for it aboard the mules of Martinez, if he ever caught up with them. So he hung on to the damned thing as he jogged on through knee-high clouds of gritty ash. He still had to get his people back to their own lines, and a guy just never knew when a machine gun might come in handy.

By midnight a confused account of Captain Gringo's attack had been wired to Mexico City, and Mexico City, or rather, the man who ran it, wasn't at all happy to learn he'd lost two trains, a battery of artillery, and more men than even a ruthless dictator could replace on short notice. So El Presidente Diaz told the blonde in bed with him to stop fooling around, for God's sake, as he yelled into his bedside telephone, "I don't give a damn what Intelligence says Captain Gringo is doing over to the east! Nobody else the other side has working for them could fuck so many things up in so few minutes! I *told* you assholes to watch out for him when I learned he was working for Guatemala!"

The general on the other end of the line said soothingly, "He has gone back up into the sierras, El Presidente, and next time he tries anything he will find we have all the passes zeroed with our big guns!"

Diaz snapped, "How do you know that crazy Yanqui is in the sierras? He has never sent us a postcard to date! I told you before and I am telling you now that the maniac is *never* where he's supposed to be!"

"His band last fired on us from west of the tracks, El Presidente. We naturally sent out combat patrols as soon as we stopped shelling his last known position. They found nothing between the tracks and the hills. Ergo, he must have retreated up into them, no?"

The crafty old dictator thought, shook his head, and said, "You forget I began my career as a guerrilla leader under

Juarez, General. If that sneaky Captain Gringo let you know he was heading west, he was really planning to be somewhere *else* by the dawn's early light! Attention to orders. I want at least a brigade, with a battery of heavy artillery, to search to the *east* for the bastard. I want *two* brigades and *four* artillery batteries to move north in case, God forbid, he's headed *this* way!"

"But, El Presidente, what about our invasion of Guatemala?"

"Fuck Guatemala. I'd rather have Captain Gringo's head on a platter! We've barely recovered from the last time he and that homicidal little Frenchman passed through Mexico a few months ago, and they both *owe* me!"

He stared absently down at the naked blonde beside him and added in a calmer tone, "We can grab some of Guatemala later, after we've eliminated their secret weapon, Captain Gringo. With their junta divided, they're in no position to stop us when we get around to them again. But let's not waste time talking. Get those soldados de fortuna. That's an order!"

He hung up, sighed, and told the blonde she'd have to start all over. So a beautiful blonde was going down on one dirty old man while, far to the south in Guatemala City, another dirty old man was giving a pretty girl an even harder time.

Evita Barrios wasn't blowing the CO of the Guatemalan army as they faced each other, fully dressed, in his office at GHQ. Evita licked her lips and asked, "Why have I been brought here under guard, Tío Eduardo?"

The general leaned back in his chair and finished lighting his cigar before he mused, "That's true, you are my naughty niece by marriage and your mother was a Cabrera, too. Obviously it would cause quite a scandal if I had you shot at dawn."

Evita blanched and stammered, "Shot? At dawn? For why, Tío Eduardo?"

He blew smoke out his nostrils like an angry bull, but kept his voice calm and reasonable as he said, "I had you arrested because there are still a few loose ends I hope you can explain to me, Señora Barrios. To save us both a lot of tedious sparring, my counterintelligence has picked up Ramon Garcia, your so-called footman and secret lover."

She laughed incredulously and asked, "Whatever gave you such an odd idea, Tío Eduardo? That peon boy means nothing to me, I assure you! If he's said wicked things about me, I demand the chance to confront him!"

The general said, "Oh, hell, we shot him hours ago. But before we did, we, ah, persuaded him to talk. But I would hardly see fit to arrest a highborn woman such as yourself just for a little French loving from a servant. No, Señora Barrios, the charges are murder and high treason."

"Oh, no!" she wailed.

But the general held up a hand for silence and said, "I have not finished. Naturally you will not face trial in open court. You know too much and you have too many relatives and no doubt lovers in both rival factions of the junta. You have my word you will not be executed or even sent to prison, provided you fill in a few missing details of the plot."

"I know nothing of any plot against you, Tío Eduardo."

The old man looked disgusted and said, "I could forgive a plot against *myself,* you wicked child. But you, a Guatemalan woman of good family, plotted with Mexico against your own country!"

"I swear to God, Tío Eduardo . . ." she began.

But he shut her up and snapped, "Do not put your immortal soul in jeopardy by swearing to lies in the name of

God. You have *enough* to answer to before the throne of your maker!"

She began to cry. It didn't work. The general's eyes were cold as ice as he said, "Since you persist in this stupid innocent act, I shall begin at the beginning, so you will know how few secrets I really want from you now."

He took a drag on his cigar, blew it out his nose again, and said, "Once upon a time there was a naughty little girl named Evita who was used to having anything she wanted, when she wanted it. One of the things this spoiled child took a fancy to was a dashing colonel in the army. He was a little old for her. He already had a wife he was devoted to, but no matter. A little poison at a social tea took care of the first Señora Barrios and in no time at all the naughty little girl was married to the widower she was consoling so kindly."

"Tío Eduardo! That is a monstrous lie!"

"No, it was a monstrous crime. Never poison anyone with any heavy metal, Señora Barrios. We've just exhumed the first wife, along with your late husband. Both cadavers were as messy as one would imagine, by now, but bismuth, being a metal, does not decay at all."

"It can't be true! In any case, even if they *were* poisoned, it was not *me,* I swear!"

The old man smiled sardonically and asked, "Did I say anything about the coroner finding traces of bismuth in your husband's bones? We are getting ahead of the story. But no matter. As you know, once the spoiled little girl found herself married to a man old enough to be her father, she began to have second thoughts. How he failed to please her is not important. Suffice it to say she poisoned him as well and, as a rich widow, was free to indulge herself with younger men, including a most handsome footman who no doubt tickled her fancy with his amazingly long tongue. Or does it work another way, Señora Barrios? Could he have blackmailed you into acting as his lover and fellow Mexican spy, knowing you had poisoned the master of the house?"

She didn't answer as her eyes rolled wildly in her pretty face.

He said, "Don't try anything silly. All the doors and windows are locked, I assure you. Let us go on to some parts of the story you may not know. Your footman was, as you know and he just confessed, an agent of our friendly neighbors to the north. He was using you both as a plaything and a tool. You were very useful to Mexico, both as a source of gossip and the spreader of gossip Diaz wished for to plant among our social circles here in the capital. Then, just as all was going well, our young friend Captain Gringo arrived on your doorstep, hiding from British agents with their own axes to grind. You had to take him and the old Frenchman in. Your footman, of course, had to go back to playing servant. He must have been most annoyed. He became more annoyed, and frightened, when that big Yanqui somehow wound up in bed with you, with your servant listening at the keyhole. He told us he heard something about poison. Was that why you dragged Captain Gringo into bed, or did you simply desire a change?"

She buried her face in her hands, now crying real tears.

The old man shrugged and said, "No matter. Your footman and fellow spy was afraid his number was up, once you'd hopped into bed with a better-looking man. He'd already tried to buy some time by telling the two soldiers of fortune a mad story about the house being watched. That, of course, was to keep them pinned down until he could decide his next move. Once you'd betrayed him with another man, and knowing what a poor liar you were, he decided desperate measures were called for. He left the house, contacted other Mexican agents, and tried to get rid of you as well as your unsettling guests in a rather dramatic manner. When even a cannon failed to shut your pretty mouth, he simply bolted and ran. My boys caught him. It was yourself who'd suggested he was acting oddly for a faithful servant. We did not know, until we'd pulled out a few fingernails, that he was a Mexican spy. But now we do. So it's your move, Señora Barrios!''

She sobbed and said, ''Please don't hurt me! I am only a weak woman! I know nothing more than you about Ramon, if the little brute betrayed me, too!''

The general said, ''You know how much of this business about a feud between the Barrios and Cabrera factions is true, and how much malicious gossip has been deliberately spread by enemies of your country, Señora Barrios. So now you are going to tell me, like a good little girl, what in the devil is going on!''

She sniffed and said, ''I know nothing of a plot by one faction or the other. Ramon said to, ah, mention it to people at social gatherings. He said things would go easier on all concerned if Guatemala did not resist the Mexican claims to the north and . . .''

''Bueno, I see it all now!'' the general cut in, adding, ''And to think even British Intelligence bought the story! Oh, well, now that I know I can trust all my senior officers with troops and guns, it may not be too late to salvage the situation.''

He rose and said, ''But I must get to work on the matter at once. So you must forgive me if I have to leave you alone here.''

He opened a desk drawer, took out a small brown bottle, and placed it on the desk between them, saying, ''If I were you, I would drink this. My surgeon general tells me no pain is involved. You will merely fall asleep in a few minutes, and, naturally, the papers will be told it was a sudden, unsuspected heart condition. So there will be no scandal."

Evita gasped and asked, "Are you suggesting I kill myself?"

He shrugged and said, "Not suggesting, ordering, unless you'd rather die in a slower, more painful manner."

"But, Tío Eduardo, you promised I would not be executed!"

He nodded and said, "You won't be. For reasons of state, you are going to die of a heart attack, with or without your cooperation. You have until I return to think it over, Señora Barrios. If you are still alive when I return . . . Well, just make sure you are *not*, eh?"

Sunrise caught Captain Gringo trudging wearily across an ashy field of dead corn. But the volcanic fallout wasn't as bad this far east, and he saw trees ahead still in full leaf. So he headed for them. He'd about given up on Gaston and the others. By now they should have veered south. That was the way *he* meant to go, once he reached cover. He looked back and saw that he was leaving one hell of an easy trail to follow in the soft gray ash.

Again he considered dropping the useless machine gun and again he hung on to it as he trudged on toward the tree line. He stiffened as he spotted movement in the greenery ahead. Then he laughed with sick relief as Gaston stepped out in the open to wave him the rest of the way in.

He dropped the Maxim and followed it to the cool forest duff under the trees as he saw the others reclining in the shade all around. Gaston hunkered down beside him and presented him with a canteen, saying, "We've been wondering what was keeping you, Dick. I have been a busy bee myself, since last we met." He turned and called out, "Lopez, bring those prisoners over here poco tiempo, hein?"

Carmella and Alicia got to Captain Gringo first and hugged him between them, kissing him on both cheeks, as he grinned and muttered, "Decisions, decisions; hold the thought, muchachas. What prisoners are we talking about, Gaston?"

The Frenchman said, "They say they are woodcutters. Here they come now."

Sergeant Lopez frog-marched a pair of shabby frightened peones over and Gaston said, "Tell our commander what you told me earlier this morning, you lying bastards."

One of the frightened woodcutters removed his battered straw sombrero and said, "We do not lie, Señores. For why would we lie? It is of no importance to us where those other people are going or what they are doing in these parts. We simply ran this way when we saw many mounted men with many guns. Had we known *you* were here with guns, we might not have run so far, eh? We are simple woodcutters. We have no business with armed people on serious business!"

Captain Gringo asked Gaston if they'd been frisked. The Frenchman nodded and said, "Oui; no ID, and the only weapons they had were the machetes they said they only used on trees."

Captain Gringo looked up at the woodcutters, if that was what they were, and asked, "How many riders in that other party and were they wearing uniforms like ours?"

"Who counts?" The more talkative peon sighed, adding, "There were many of them, with guns. We ran. We did not even untether our poor burros. They were not in any kind of uniform at all, Señor. They looked like desperados. Big loud men with big loud guns. One was dressed in white and rode a white horse."

Gaston frowned thoughtfully and suggested, "Caballero Blanco, Dick?"

Captain Gringo said, "More like irregulars scouting for los federales. No bandit with any sense rides anywhere near los federales without a hunting license. They're probably after *us*."

The peon who hadn't spoken yet said, "They were surely after *someone*, Señor! As they passed us I heard one shouting something about gringo bastards."

The two soldiers of fortune exchanged glances. Captain Gringo nodded and said, "So much for heading south, this close to that railhead. Does anyone here have any idea what's due east?"

One of the local peones nodded and said, "Sí; condado malo, Señor. Thick cut-over brush, where it is not true jungle, and all cut up by the drainage north into Mexico. You could not get through there with your mules. Those other riders were on the only reasonable route into the lowlands."

Captain Gringo took a swig from the canteen, shoved his adelitas far enough apart to breathe, for God's sake, and said, "Bueno. If you can't take mules that way, nobody will be expecting us to."

Gaston said, "Eh bien, but how are *we* supposed to punch our way through an adorable jungle cut up by ravines, my dauntless explorer?"

"We have these two guides, right?"

The captured woodcutters blanched collectively and told him he had to be kidding. One said, "Por favor, Señor, we do not know the way, even if we were crazy enough to *go* that way. Did I forget to mention there are bad Indios in the jungles to the east as well?"

Captain Gringo grimaced and said, "You just did." Then he got back to his feet and said, "We'd better get cracking, gang. By now some wise-ass Mexican cavalry scout is sure to have cut the trail I left leading right to here. So let's get the show on the road again!''

As he started shouting orders to saddle up, Gaston asked what about the woodcutters, and the tall American said, "Let 'em go. Unwilling guides who don't know the way can get you in more trouble than just guessing.''

"True, but they are liable to tell our Mexican friends which way we went, non?''

"Shit, if los federales can't figure that out for themselves, they need a refresher course in I and R. Let 'em go back for their burros. I mean it, Gaston. I don't want you being pratique behind a tree with the poor bastards.''

"Spoilsport,'' muttered Gaston.

Mattinez came over, saluted, and said he was glad to see that Captain Gringo had made it and that he was awaiting orders. So Captain Gringo asked him if he had wax in his ears and added that the Maxim he'd lugged all the way could use a shave and a haircut, next trail break. Martinez asked when that might be and the American shrugged and said, "Next time we get stuck, I guess. Right now I want to put as much distance as I can between us and those sons of bitches trying to cut us off!''

The next few days were a confusing High Road–Low Road situation as Captain Gringo and the outraged forces of El Presidente Diaz tried to outmaneuver one another in ever-thickening rain forest. The Mexicans kept pushing east via the High Road or, rather, the only sensible route through a tangle that kept getting worse by the mile, while Cabellero Blanco, scouting ahead for them, kept trying to cut north

across the Guatemalan line of retreat and, failing, assuring his
Mexican masters that it was impossible to get a horse through
stuff that looked like giant spinach armed with thorns. Cabellero
Blanco was right, even though the Mexican officers cursed
him and ordered him to try harder. Captain Gringo and his
people never could have gotten *horses* through the way they
were moving, north of the federales, but a mule could go
anywhere a human could go, if the human cursed and pleaded
hard enough.

It was impossible to move nearly a full regiment with its
women and baggage through some stretches silently, of course,
and the sounds of machetes and falling trees carried for miles
in the rain-forest gloom. Every time the Mexicans heard the
crash of wood in the distance they lobbed a couple of shells
in its general direction for luck. So, though they never hit
near enough to matter, the progress of both parties was pretty
noisy and each had a general idea about where the other
might be at any given moment. Gaston decided he'd had
about enough of this one-sided shelling. During a trail break,
he unlimbered an antique mountain gun and tried an experi-
ment. He knew that lobbing canister shot up and over the
trees was a waste of powder. So he charged the muzzle
loader, shoved a length of dry balsa stalk he'd found down the
smooth bore, and poured lamp oil down after it to soak into
the porous wood awhile before he crossed his fingers and
fired.

The results were probably harmless but dramatic. The
oil-soaked length of balsa sailed over some federales to the
south, whirling like a boomerang, screaming like a banshee,
and flaming like a pinwheel to spook their horses and make
them wonder what in the hell *that* had been.

Captain Gringo told Gaston to cut the comedy as the
enemy to their south returned the insult with an expensive

barrage that, fortunately, landed far beyond them, smashing up a couple of acres of good furniture wood and scaring the living crap out of a troop of howler monkeys.

The howlers were not the only inhabitants of the jungle frightened by the noisy progress of the opposing forces. Unreconstructed Indians, mostly Garifuna or Quechua Maya, had no idea who in the hell was lobbing shells into the treetops all around them and didn't wait to find out. Thus, as Captain Gringo tried to outdistance the Mexicans, without much luck because of the rougher going ahead of him, he was preceded eastward by a screen of bewildered primitives he didn't even know about.

It was just as well for all concerned. The Quechua Maya were tough enough, albeit more cultivated than the truculent Garifuna, who tended to attack strangers coming at them in more reasonable numbers. One afternoon Caballero Blanco did find a game trail leading north across Captain Gringo's line of retreat. But when two of his muchachos took reed arrows tipped with poison from the surrounding underbrush, he decided not to mention the trail to his Mexican masters, and, since the main column passed it after sundown, they missed a swell chance to kill Indians and cut off Captain Gringo.

The Garifuna, in turn, had moved farther east by the time Captain Gringo led his own column across the trail and plunged on into the green hell ahead. As the now soggy forest floor dropped ever lower toward the coastal swamps, they found themselves in a jackstraw maze of wind-felled mahogany, logwood, campeachy, and corozo palms, laced together by thorny vines and guarded by red ants and invisible hissing whatevers glaring out of the woodpile at them.

He knew it would take forever, and make too much noise, to cut a trail through that way. He led his column around, via a log-dammed swamp where the mules sank to their bellies in tea-colored water and mosquitoes hung thick as smoke to serenade and torment them as, overhead, howlers cursed and shit on them. It took them the better part of a day to work their way back to dry land, pitch tents, and call it a day. Meanwhile, Mexican scouts tougher than Caballero Blanco had found the Indian trail leading to the far side of the windfall, been as convinced that it was impassable, and reported back that whichever way the crazy gringo was going, it had to be another. The federale brigadier ordered a barrage laid around the woodpile anyway. He had orders, for God's sake, to do *something* about Captain Gringo.

The distant drumfire was sort of soothing to the big Yank as he lay in his tent, naked between his two adelitas, a little too tired to roll atop either, but enjoying their comforting presence as the redhead kissed him while her mulatto companion played with them both.

Meanwhile, farther to the east, the British expedition up the Rio Hondo had run, if not out of steam, out of deep enough water for an armored gunboat to navigate. The commander of the force, yet another brigadier, decided that this stretch of the south branch of the Hondo would do as well as anywhere for the new border of British Honduras.

He called in an aide and said, "We'll build our outpost here, Major. Head of navigation, good spot for a trading post and all that, what?"

The aide nodded but asked, "How far further west would the general like his forward OPs?"

"OPs? Don't bother, Major. Happen to know this area is not inhabited. Reason we've claimed it for Her Majesty, eh what?"

The aide hesitated and said, "Begging the general's pardon, Intelligence reports quite a few pagan Indians in the woods all about."

The brigadier shrugged and said, "I know. Read the perishing reports myself. Of course there are Indians, Major. No point in a trading post here if there were no bloody Indians. They'll no doubt be glad to be taken under the protection of the Union Jack. The Mosquito Indians further south asked for our protection against the flaming dago Nicaraguans, what?"

"I know our excuse for liberating the Mosquito Coast from Bluefields to Greytown, Sir. But neither the local Garifuna nor Quechua Maya have asked for our intervention in these parts."

"Balderdash, Major. Whitehall knows what's best for the little red buggers. They have nothing to say about it if we want to liberate 'em. All for their own good, of course. Would you want to live under dago Guatemalans when you could be a British subject?"

"Of course not, General, but from what I hear, the wilder tribes in these parts may not grasp the full advantages of British civilization. The Garifuna, ah, shoot poison arrows even at other Indians."

"We'll worry about their manners after we hoist the Union Jack and erect our stockade ashore. The blighters will doubtless see reason, once we've offered them tobacco and salt. May have to shoot a few of the stubborn ones. Can't be helped. It's our duty to protect the naked bastards from exploitation, what?"

He moved to a porthole, gazed out it with the contented expression of a country squire, and said, "I want the marine engineers to start at once, over there in that stand of logwood.

May as well have some profit while we're clearing the ground, eh what?''

The aide frowned and asked, "Are we setting up on the *west* bank, Sir? I thought the Hondo here was to be our new border with Guatemala.''

"Borders are open to continued negotiation, Major, and the bank on that side's higher and drier. I say, is that *thunder* I hear?''

The aide cocked his head to listen before he said, "Sounds more like artillery fire to me, Sir.''

The brigadier shook his head and said, "Nonsense. Thunder. Our Intelligence says no Guatemalan forces are anywhere near here. The dons are having some sort of interfamily feud and can't come out to play until they settle it. By then we'll be well set up along this new border, and, you'll see, they won't do anything dramatic. They're still bitching about our last adjustment of the border, but they'll just talk.''

The aide didn't argue, even though the sunset sky outside was rather clear for the dull rumbles he kept hearing in the distance. He asked, "Does the general think it wise to start the engineers working in gathering darkness with a possible thunderstorm approaching?''

The brigadier laughed and said, "You must be new to the tropics, Major. That thunder's off to our west. The prevailing trades are blowing that way, too. Ergo, the perishing thunder's not coming our way. It's going the *other* way. As for the lads working in the dark, any old tropic hand can tell you it beats working under the bloody *sun* down here!''

The aide saluted and said he'd get right to it. Out in the gangway he met a marine officer and said, "Well, your lot's in for it, Jim. The old man wants the stockade started at once. You have the plans. Standard outpost. Only change is that he wants the bloody thing on the west bank, not the east.''

The marine frowned and said, "Coo, that leaves us in a sticky wicket should we have to retreat, doesn't it?"

The aide smiled thinly and said, "Royal Marines do not retreat, Captain."

The marine said, "Mayhaps not, but sometime we have to make a *strategic withdrawal* in one hell of a hurry! We still haven't heard from the bloody Yanks about this latest move by Whitehall, Major."

"That's because their President Cleveland isn't supposed to know about it until it's a fait accompli, old boy. Their grotesque Monroe Doctrine does not apply to *established* European colonies on their side of the pond. They merely seem a bit uffish about conquests they notice *ahead* of time."

The marine shrugged and said, "Ours is not to reason why, I suppose. But this could still wind up a sticky mess if Guatemala and the Yanks ganged up on us."

"Don't worry, there can't be a Guatemalan or a Yank within miles of this bloody river."

By sunrise the British expeditionary force had the Union Jack waving above a pretty imposing outpost of the empire. Despite their commanding officer's overconfidence, the junior naval and marine officers, or, to be more accurate, the enlisted men under them, had built a log stockade with a blockhouse at each corner out of a king's ransom worth of tropical hardwood. At least a dining-room set and a grandfather clock could have been carved out of many a mahogany log facing the unknown. The Royal Marines were more interested in their bullet-stopping properties.

To make things even harder for anyone less than enthusiastic about the new borders of British Honduras, they'd cleared a field of fire three hundred yards wide around the outpost. They mounted a machine gun in each corner blockhouse, and the gunboat moored behind the layout offered the fire of its two armored gun turrets for anyone who couldn't be convinced by four machine guns and a demibrigade's repeating rifles. The steam launches the Royal Marines had come upstream aboard had been run ashore under the riverside walls of the stockade. The brigadier was so pleased with his men's work that he ordered a general inspection, full dress, for noon, sharp.

Less than five miles to the west, Captain Gringo of course had no idea that anyone but los federales was near enough to matter as he woke up in his tent in the jungle, kissed Alicia good morning, and told Carmella to let go of his poor tired dong for God's sake. It was getting light enough to read the map and that was more important right now, dammit.

He got dressed and crawled out into the morning mist to see other early risers at work. He told the adelitas preparing to fix breakfast not to build any fires, explaining that they were too close to the south fork of the Rio Hondo to risk smoke above the treetops. Then he sat on a tree that wasn't standing tall anymore and took out his map to study it. It wasn't easy. The sun was still low, and even when it was high, above jungle canopy, the leaves above made the jungle floor as gloomy as the interior of a chicken coop. He sort of wished he were *in* a chicken coop instead of a lowland jungle right now. A chicken coop smelled nicer than the rotting vegetation and monkey shit all around, and there might not have been as many bugs.

He brushed a fuzzy green spider off the map and decided that he and his followers were just about . . . *here*, give or take an error of a mile or so. Gaston came to join him, buttoning his fly, and sat down at his side, saying, "I can't stand early risers. But some freaks of nature will insist on waking up filled with beans.''

Captain Gringo said, ''I'm not full of beans. I could sleep until noon if I thought those fucking federales were at least out of artillery range.''

Gaston said, ''I was not talking about you. That damned Rosita wanted me to eat her for breakfast, before I was *awake!* Merde alors, common courtesy is one thing, but an unwashed pussy under one's sleeping nose wakes one up faster than smelling salts. What *other* disgusting plans have you for us today, oh great explorer?''

''First we'd better put out some scouts. There's open ground ahead of us, no more than a few miles.''

Gaston said, ''It's been done. I sent out dawn patrols before dawn. I had to do *something* when I told my oversexed adelitas I was too busy to take care of two women at once.''

''I know the feeling. So how come you were just buttoning up your pants?''

''Sacrebleu, I have been awake almost an hour. Once a man washes the sleep from his eyes and has a smoke, two women at once are not bad. Tell me more about this open ground ahead of us. If you are talking about the south fork of the Hondo, somewhere ahead, forget it. You should know by now that the spinach grows thicker along an open waterway than anywhere else in the jungle, hein?''

Captain Gringo drew Gaston's attention to a faint line on the somewhat mildewed map and said, ''I'm not talking about the river ahead. This contour line spells a shallow rise between us and the Hondo. Rubber tappers always follow the high ground. So there's sure to be at least a foot trail running, *so*, between us and the river. The river's where we want to go. It's barely fordable, ahead. We can get across with our mules. Los rurales can get across with their horses. But they'll have a time getting their big field guns over to the other side."

"It's not impossible to drag big guns across anything, in time, Dick."

"Sure, but while they're *taking* time, we'll be *making* time. See how the ground rises on the far side of the Hondo? The high ground runs north and south. If we can only get a few hours' lead on the Mexicans we'll be in the clear. We can beeline down to San Lorenzo and fort up with the Guatemalan garrison there if los federales want to chase us that far. They probably won't. Either way, we'll have our people home free."

Gaston nodded, but said, "I have an even better plan. We still have a little money, our sidearms, and our civilian clothing in our packs, non?"

"Sure. So what?"

"So what if we simply showed our adorable children the way home and built ourselves a balsa when we got to the Hondo? It would offer us a free ride down to the seaport of Corozal in British Honduras. We know the town, we both speak English, and any number of tramp steamers bound for Costa Rica put in at Corozal, non?"

"God damn it, Gaston, you heard me tell the others I'd shoot anyone who deserted in the face of the enemy!"

"True, but who is likely to shoot you and me?"

Before Gaston could continue, Sergeant Lopez ran up to them, out of breath, to report, "Our scouts just came in. We've been cut off ahead! There is a wide trail between us and the next river valley, Señores, and those irregulars scouting for the Mexicans have *found* it!"

Captain Gringo muttered, "Shit, I wish they didn't issue maps to everybody. Are they dug in or just patrolling across out front, Lopez?"

"Both, Captain Gringo! The guerrillas are riding back and forth, as if looking for an easy way through the jungle wall. Some federale infantry has moved up the trail as well, and, sí, they are starting to dig foxholes right on the trail!"

Captain Gringo studied his map one last time for luck, stood up, and said, "Gather the other officers for me, Lopez. *Quietly,* por favor."

As they waited, Gaston said, "If they had us pinpointed, they would be shelling us, non?"

The American replied, "Give the bastards time. At least we know where *they* are!"

"Only their advance units, Dick. The main body is still flanking us to the south. That leaves us north or west to move, très suddenly!"

Captain Gringo shook his head and said, "Wrong. I want to get us *out* of these fucking woods, not deeper into them! We'll be okay, once we're across the Hondo. So that's where we'll go."

"Merde alors, are you still asleep, Dick? The man just said both irregulars and regulars are dug in to wait for us, this side of your très fatigué river crossing!"

As he saw his junior leaders approaching, he nodded grimly and said, "Yeah, so let's not keep 'em waiting until they've really beefed up their line."

As the others assembled around him, Captain Gringo explained the situation and added, "I don't have time to inspire the troops with another speech. So each of you will have to. They'll rake us if we hit 'em in column. So we'll attack broadside, soldados in the first line of skirmish with the adelitas following, leading two mules each. Martinez, you and me will advance on either flank, with our two machine guns. Can you fire a Maxim from the hip?"

Martinez shrugged and said, "I have never tried. I may be able to, if I have to."

"You'll have to. I'll take the right flank, you take the left. Gaston here will lead the middle."

Gaston snorted wearily and asked, "Why are you so good to me? Can I at least leave those toy cannon behind?"

Captain Gringo started to nod. Then he asked, "Gaston, could you train those little buggers south, with delayed fuses firing them, oh, half an hour after nobody's home, here?"

Gaston grinned like a mean little kid and said, "Oui, if I build a slow smudge fire for each, with the fuse on the bottom. I see your plan, and since my adorable derriere won't be anywhere near them when they go off, I shall take the liberty of overcharging the guns. You do want them thinking we are bombarding them with serious weapons, non?"

"Yeah; if they send counterbattery into an abandoned camp, they won't be lobbing shells at *us*. Not as many anyway. You'd better get cracking. We're moving out in fifteen minutes. You other guys, synchronize your watches. I'm not waiting for any jerk-offs who can't tell time."

Less than an hour later, the British brigadier and his aide were somewhat startled to hear all hell breaking loose beyond the tree wall to their west as they stood atop the catwalk of the stockade. The brigadier said, "I say, that sounds like gunfire, eh what?"

His aide said, "It does, Sir, and some of it's automatic fire. Battle stations?"

"Eh, what? Battle stations? Oh, right, better have the lads man the loopholes and all that. Does sound like a perishing lot of small-arms fire over that way."

Then, as Gaston's abandoned mountain guns roared louder than they'd ever been meant to roar, he amended it to, "By Jove, some blighter's firing bloody *artillery!*"

He was not alone in his observation. A few miles to the south, a startled Mexican artillery officer hit the dirt as one of Gaston's whirling lengths of cordwood whizzed over him, sounding exactly like at least an eight-inch shell. He didn't notice that it failed to detonate as it crashed into the treetops farther south. He leaped to his feet and bellowed, "Counterbattery fire at will, you triple-thumbed motherfuckers! What are you *waiting* for!"

His gunnery sergeant saluted nervously and asked, "What is our point of aim, My Captain?"

The officer roared, "What point of aim, you asshole? They're firing at us from somewhere in that fucking jungle to the north. I want a harassing barrage laid down all over that part of the world and I want it *now!*"

So the Mexican heavies opened up, all along the line, to send shell after shell screaming blindly in a wide fan of destruction, and, while the first few rounds didn't hit anyone, they scared the wits out of everyone north of the main Mexican advance and south of Captain Gringo's more modest but no less deadly one. The Guatemalan troopers and the Mexicans they were advancing against at least knew what an artillery shell was. The poor Garifuna Indians between the dug-in Mexicans and the river were simply scared shitless and ran through the trees for the river in blind but also enraged panic.

Up on the catwalk of the stockade, the brigadier and his aide were still in the same place as, the bugle having blown, Royal Marines fell into place at loopholes around them. The aide spotted the Indians popping out of the trees to the west first and nudged his commander, saying, "We seem to have company, Sir."

The brigadier turned, saw the hundred or so howling Garifuna coming his way, and said, "Ah, no doubt the poor blighters are running to us for protection, eh what?"

"Begging the general's pardon, they don't look too friend-ly at the moment!"

He was correct in his assumption. The Indians skidded to a confused stop, still lined up with their bows and arrows, as they saw that they were cut off from the river crossing by yet *more* of the noisy rude strangers who'd invaded their hunting grounds!

A Mexican shell went off in the jungle behind them, making them all jump forward a few paces. Then, just as their chief barked an order to cut around the mysterious new clearing in their path, another shell landed, close, and some Indian muttered the Garifuna version of, "What the hell?" and shot a six-foot reed arrow at the stockade. The others thought that was a swell suggestion, and even as the brigadier was shouting, "Open fire, dammit!" an arrow among many arched down to bury its poisoned tip in his chest!

The brigadier muttered, "Oh, I say," as his aide caught him and shouted to the nearest marines, "Carry him back to the gunboat. Tell the skipper I want some rounds along that tree line and . . ." Then a big Mexican shell landed in the open between him and the Indians, knocking a dozen of them flat. So he changed it to, "Tell the skipper to range on those flaming big guns! The blighters are shooting at *us* now!"

Deeper in the jungle, Captain Gringo and his followers naturally assumed that any big bangs ahead of them were Mexican shells, aimed blind. So they ignored them as they worried more about the smaller guns they knew were between them and the river they had to reach.

The federales hadn't finished digging in yet along the trail as the Guatemalan skirmish line burst out of the brush at them, laying down a fusillade of marching fire.

Los federales held their ground as best they could. They simply couldn't hold it good enough. Captain Gringo and Martinez complicated their lives further by hosing automatic fire at them from both flanks of the wide Guatemalan advance, making more than one man they missed hug the ground more than was wise, with guys closer charging in with carbines. Some who looked up in time caught bullets with their startled faces. Others were hit in the ass as they tried to burrow deeper into the red clay. It wasn't funny when it happened to you.

Captain Gringo's people took some fatal bullets, too. Some of the federales were good soldados. More of them, if they were still able, cut and ran as their positions were steamrolled.

By then, of course, Caballero Blanco and his irregulars had already been running for some time. So the Royal Marines had no sooner seen the last of the "attacking Indians" than they were faced with what seemed to be a mass of mounted mestizos charging out of the jungle at them!

They did what any Royal Marines would do at such a distressing time. They opened up on the guerrillas without waiting for orders, and, as saddle after saddle emptied and some few guerrillas even managed to return the fire in their confusion, the aide, who'd taken over from the dying expedition commander, was not at all displeased that his men were firing at will.

One still on a white horse was shouting something that sounded like defiance as he rode toward the fort, waving his big white sombrero. So the aide drew his service revolver, braced it on the stockade, and blew away Caballero Blanco, growling, "Yell at *me*, will you, you perishing dago!"

Meanwhile, on the river, the gunners aboard the ironclad had zeroed on the distant Mexican field guns to the south with their masthead range finder. So the next time the Mexican gunners had to duck, it was real incoming mail. One field gun was laid on its side like a dead cow with its crew hash-browned all around. The Mexican artillery commander was not easily frightened. He just got mad as hell and told his own range finders to for God's sake *do* something!

So they did, and in no time at all Mexico and Great Britain were engaged in a vicious artillery duel over the heads of Captain Gringo and his followers.

They had no more idea who was firing heavy rounds at whom than the people firing them did. But it seemed like a good time to lie flat on the ground between the trees and hope like hell nobody had *them* pinpointed!

As he kept his people down, midway between the Mexican line they'd overrun and the British lines they didn't even know about, Captain Gringo ordered a head count.

It could have been worse, but it could have been better, and he had to swallow hard to keep from puking when he learned how expensive his attack had been. They'd lost thirty-seven men, twenty-four mules, and a dozen adelitas. Gaston tried to put it gently when he had to report that two of the missing and presumed dead were Carmella and Alicia.

Captain Gringo took a gulp of air, let half of it out so his voice wouldn't crack, and asked, "Did anyone actually see them buy the farm?"

Gaston shook his head and said, "No. But the one mule of yours that made it was badly cut up and had to be destroyed. I told them to put your saddle on another. It is not as if we had none to spare now."

Captain Gringo pounded the ground with his fist and said, "Dammit, Gaston, there was no other way!"

"Eh bien, I was there, my old and rare. Listen to those shells come down like rain! From the damage to your mule, I'd say it was a wild artillery round that took out the other mule and the girls. But I can't make my head from my tail what on earth is going on! Those idiots must be aiming at *something*, non?"

Captain Gringo cocked his head and listened before he replied, "I can't make heads or tails out of it either. It sounds like someone's sending and receiving mail from the river crossing ahead. The other guns are firing somewhere to our south, and being fired on, too! Did you ever get the feeling you were not alone in the house?"

"Oui; if we are listening to an artillery duel, and I can't think what else it could be, a third party would seem to have joined the fun and games, non?"

Martinez crawled over to join them, saying, "The others are awaiting further orders, Captain Gringo."

The American said, "Tell 'em to just sit tight until I figure what the hell is going on. It's starting to look as if the Mexican main column cut us off from the river, dammit. But now someone to the south is firing on them. Could be other Guatemalan forces. There's a garrison at San Lorenzo, right?"

"Sí, but I did not know they had big guns. It is only a border post. A company of riflemen. Not very good ones."

Gaston asked, "What about the main Guatemalan army, Dick?"

The American said, "Makes more sense than anything else I can think of. If the junta's settled its differences, somehow, they could have sent a demonstration of force up here to block that rumor about a British land grab."

Gaston chuckled and said, "Eh bien, how droll. Perhaps they don't even know they are shooting at Mexicans. They may think they are firing at some wandering band of British. I wonder who the Mexicans think they are firing at. Both sides are burning up a très formidable amount of expensive ammunition, hein?''

Actually, both los federales and the British expeditionary force were finding their blind artillery duel expensive in more ways than one. At the stockade, a wounded marine officer stared numbly down at the mangled remains of the brigadier's aide as other marines formed a bucket brigade to fight the fire in one badly shattered blockhouse. A noncom covered with red dust and a badly torn uniform came up to him, saluted, and said, ''Sir! Scouts report recovering the body of a dead Mexican officer a quarter mile inside the tree line.''

The marine officer frowned and asked, ''Don't you mean *Guatemalan,* Sergeant? We were told the Guats might kick up a bit of a fuss, although I must say this is more fuss than we bargained for.''

The noncom shook his head and insisted, ''Here's his pay book, Major. As you can see, we've potted a Lieutenant Fernandez, Federal Army of The United States of Mexico!''

The marine officer sighed and said, ''That tears it, then. The only way the United States of Mexico would have the balls to attack Her Majesty's forces would be with the backing of the better-known United States to the bloody north! I've been afraid from the start that the bloody Yanks would stick their bloody noses into this little real-estate transaction!''

The sergeant just stood there, waiting for orders. The now senior commander of the badly shot-up British expedition knew he was expected to give some order or other. It hurt like hell, but it had to be done. He said, ''We'll have to pull out. Some civilian twit at Whitehall's made a perishing bloody mistake and we've paid enough for it. Pass the word, no dead or wounded are to be left behind. We evacuate in half an hour. Carry on, Sergeant!''

Miles away, as gunboat shells continued to land on the Mexican positions, and would continue to do so until the last steam launch carried its British survivors out of range down the Hondo, a federale officer wearing a bandage instead of a kepi on his head ran in a low crouch across a patch of flattened jungle to roll over a log and report to the higher-ranking but rather ragged short-colonel behind it, ''Lieutenant Valente's compliments, Sir. He says he has only two twelve-pounders left and that he's almost out of rounds as well!''

The short-colonel frowned and asked, ''For why is a lieutenant now in command of our artillery? What happened to your major?''

''Dead, Sir. The captain, too. Whoever told us those Guatemalan irregulars had no big guns to match ours was, forgive me, full of shit!''

The short-colonel shrugged and said, ''Do not speak ill of the dead. Our brigadier has more than paid for any mistakes he made. They say that little Frenchman riding with Captain Gringo used to be an artillery officer in this very army. Wherever he got those guns, he certainly knows how to use them! Have our irregular scouts brought anything new in for to put on my already confused situation map?''

''Only one made it back, badly wounded, half an hour or so ago. Before he died he gave a most confused account about riding into an ambush near the river. He said Caballero Blanco was killed, by men dug in behind a stockade, over that way!''

The short-colonel swore and said, ''Caramba, that finishes it. Obviously Captain Gringo and his irregulars have received reinforcements from the main Guatemalan army. That accounts for the pounding we've been taking, too! We'd better get out of here muy pronto!''

"But, My Colonel, we were told the divided junta would not fight!''

"Sí; we were told not to worry about heavy artillery, too, and the harmless pobrecitos have destroyed our railhead and are whittling us down to size even as we argue about it! We'd better get back to Mexico before some Guatemalan gunner gets even luckier. Headquarters has some rethinking to do about this foolproof plan of theirs. Meanwhile, *I* have to think of my wife and children!''

And so, as Captain Gringo and his command lay bemused in the jungle between them, both the British and Mexican invasion forces sullenly withdrew in different directions, each thinking it had been creamed by Guatemala.

When Gaston noted that the shelling all around them had faded away, Captain Gringo nodded and said, "Yeah, but let's not literally jump any guns just yet. We'll stay here until, oh, siesta time. Then, if nobody's started up again, you and me will take a little walk to see what we shall see, while those bastards over by the river are taking their siesta, see?''

"Merde alors, if you want one of my adelitas that much, I'll just give her to you, Dick. You don't have to get me killed.''

Captain Gringo swallowed the green taste in his mouth and growled, "I wish you wouldn't mention women before lunch, dammit.''

It hardly seemed likely that a half-ruined stockade with one blockhouse burning would still be occupied. But Captain Gringo still told Gaston to cover him as he stepped out in the open, carbine at port, to move in across the chopped-up field of fire.

There was cover in case he needed any in a hurry. The British had left lots of tree stumps and the Mexican shelling had left lots of craters. He was somewhat confused by the first dead Indian he found in his zigzag path. The shot-up guerrilla sprawled by a dead horse on the far side of a shell crater made more sense. Both bodies were starting to bloat in the heat, and the ants and bluebottle flies had found them first. So it seemed even less likely that anyone was still holding the mysterious outpost ahead.

He came to the body of a man all in white, spread-eagled on his back to stare up at the sky as best he could with bugs crawling over his dead eyeballs. Captain Gringo grimaced down at Caballero Blanco and muttered, "This is getting monotonous, chum."

He made his way to a gap in the stockade, saw that nobody was inside, and waved Gaston out of the trees as he stepped inside. The evacuating British hadn't left anything important behind. But they hadn't bothered to police their brass. So when he picked up a spent cartridge and read "Enfield" stamped on its base, he began to grasp what could have been going on here.

Gaston joined him, with four money belts draped over one elbow, and said, "Waste not want not. Those poor Indians back there must have come out of the bushes to loot the dead a little too early. I've always found it wiser to wait until the battle is over. Any species of dead on this side of the wall, Dick?"

Captain Gringo said, "No, but their brass says they were Brits. We heard there were some of those guys over this way, remember?"

Gaston shook his head and said, "We're too far from the

border of British Honduras. Your President Cleveland would never stand for even his Tante Victoria taking *this* much real estate from his little brown brothers. The people here may have been Guatemalan rebels who got a buy on British surplus, non?''

Captain Gringo shrugged and said, ''Whoever they were, they're long gone and there's nothing to stop us from crossing the river. So let's go back and gather our flock. I want us all across the Hondo and safe on the high ground to the east before sundown.''

So they did, and by darkness the remains of Captain Gringo's irregular regiment were camped high and dry well to the southeast. They'd earned a rest and he'd lost enough eggs from his basket. So he decided to send out advance patrols, by daylight, before marching toward San Lorenzo and their just reward.

Thanks to their mostly male casualty figures, they now had more than enough adelitas to go around. So those officers and men who'd lost their original tent mates had no trouble finding new ones to console them and vice versa. Captain Gringo didn't try. He didn't have to. He'd really planned on a good night's sleep, alone for a change, in order to rest up for the march back to safety and the big payoff.

But he wasn't terribly surprised when, along about nine-thirty or ten, his tent flap opened and someone who sure smelled nice crawled in to join him, saying he could call her Teresa and adding that the man she'd lost had been an officer, too.

He said he understood how she outranked any other adelita who might have wanted to console him, and lit a cigar, not so much to smoke it as to see what he was getting into.

She was a light mestiza and beautiful, in a dumb wide-eyed way. She said, ''Oh, you are naked, Señor!''

He said, "I always take off my clothes before I go to bed. Why don't you do the same and join me?"

She fluttered her lashes and said, "Oh, this is so sudden. Did you take me for a *puta* only interested in adventures of love, Señor?"

He shook out the match and said, "Call me Dick. Did you have something else on your mind, Teresa?"

She giggled and said, "Oh, you are so forward. I might have known it would be useless to try and resist your advances. But seriously, Deek, I came for to *warn* you. Now that they have won the battle, some of the other officers are saying bad things about you."

He heard the slither of her clothes as she began to undress, so he snubbed out the barely lit cigar and muttered, "That was to be expected. Everyone knows how an attack should have been planned, once it's over."

"Sí; but now I shall tell you who is plotting against you and you can deal with the traitors, no?"

He said, "No. Someone's always griping, and we'll be safe in San Lorenzo in a day or so. So let 'em plot. It usually takes at least a couple of weeks to get a mutiny out of the bake oven. Are you bashful or something? What are you doing way over there, Teresa?"

He reached out and took her hand in the dark as she shyly answered, "I fear I do feel somewhat awkward now, Deek. I thought we would, ah, discuss the unrest in other parts of camp, ah, first."

He pulled her down beside him and took her naked body in his arms as he soothed, "Let's let them worry about it and get a little less unrested ourselves. Gee, you sure do bulge a lot for such a little thing, Teresa."

She giggled and cuddled closer before she gasped and

asked, "Madre de Dios, what is that I feel bulging against *me?*"

That was too dumb a question to bother answering. So he kissed her to shut her up and rolled atop her. She kissed back warmly, and tried to be a good sport about it when he spread her thighs and got into the usual point of entry. But as he entered her, or tried to, she whimpered and sobbed, with her lips still pressed to his, "Oh, wait, you are a bigger man than I thought! I don't think I can take all that, Deek!"

Then, as her lubrication improved with her excitement, she surrendered completely and moaned in pleasure as they discovered he could get it in after all. By then they were both so hot they made up for lost time. She raked his back with her nails and pounded his bounding buttocks with her bare heels as he pounded her, hard, in a simple old-fashioned get-together. So they knew each other a lot better by the time they'd both climaxed in each other's arms.

Between times, as she cuddled against him while he smoked, Teresa pleaded with him to make her his new official *adelita*. He said he'd think about it. He couldn't imagine how any of the other leftover camp followers could offer a guy more pleasure in the sack. But there was no sense surrendering all his options before they marched to San Lorenzo. As he'd hoped, Teresa presented some very convincing arguments before sunrise with her shapely little body as well as her pouty lips. By the time they'd worn each other out enough to opt for at least a little sleep, she'd given herself to him every way but flying, and he suspected she'd have tried that, had she had wings.

In the end, he somehow never got around to putting it in anyone else's end as he led his battered but victorious band south. Teresa was one of those passionate little hot tamales no man in his right mind would want to keep forever. But, on the other hand, she was a cute little man-eater made for at least a long warm weekend, and it only took a few days to reach San Lorenzo.

San Lorenzo was little more than a clearing in the jungle by the headwaters of the Rio Belize, another waterway leading out of Guatemala down through British Honduras. Since no Guatemalan river traffic could use the Belize enough to matter, San Lorenzo's tiny garrison had been posted there to make sure no British river steamers came that far up-stream, either, unless they wanted sniper fire through the wheelhouse. But the friendly garrison there had medics for his walking wounded and, even better, a telegraph line to Guatemala City. So as his survivors and the military and civilian population outside enjoyed their impromptu victory celebration, Captain Gringo wired a full account of their activities to date. He didn't call what had happened a victory. He was still a little confused about just what the hell *had* happened. But he informed the general that it looked like los federales were stalled and that no British seemed to be squatting in this part of Guatemala after all.

A little over an hour later, as he was seated at a trestle table in the village square, watching the fiesta continue unabated as the sun went down and paper lanterns were lit, a private from the military telegraph office brought a return message to him.

He put down his tin cup of sangría and read it by lantern light. It wasn't from the old general. It was from an aide left to hold the fort in the old man's absence. Most of the news was good. The American embassy in the capital had gotten off the dime and handed a stiff warning to the British after learning, via American agents in British Honduras, that the Royal Marines were up to something. Uncle Sam hadn't acted until he and everyone else who read newspapers had learned that said Royal Marines had just had the stuffings knocked out of them, in a part of Central America where Uncle Sam saw no reason for them to have been, with or without their stuffings intact.

Uncle Sam hadn't chided his sweet little nephew, El Presidente Diaz, about Mexico's uncouth behavior. Queen Victoria's foreign office had, rather rudely. El Presidente had publicly assured his British amigos that he most certainly did not want a war with them and protested, innocently, that anyone who claimed he was sending troops anywhere outside his borders to lob shells at anyone was a big fibber. Any men in federale uniform anyone might have seen anywhere else had to be mere banditos, no doubt wearing stolen military kit. Why would Mexico have sent real soldados to bother El Presidente's friendly neighbors to the south or east?

Captain Gringo was getting to the less pleasant news near the bottom of the telegram when Gaston staggered over to join him, feeling no pain. The little Frenchman plopped down on the bench at his side and marveled, "Eh bien, what a nice party this is. I have been propositioned by at least a dozen pretty femmes young enough to be my granddaughters, and the night has barely started!"

Captain Gringo said, "Don't get any drunker and don't shack up where I can't find you in a hurry. Now that it looks like Guatemala just won a war, cheap, guess who's coming to the party?"

Gaston looked owlishly at him, belched, and asked, "Who cares? The more the merrier, non?"

"Non. The general in person is headed this way with a full division."

Gaston shrugged and said, "So what? I just said the more the merrier, my thoughtfully frowning youth. Why are you thoughtfully frowning, Youth? If the old man's on his way here, we don't have to go all the way to Guatemala City to get paid off, hein?''

"It's the payoff I'm worried about. This wire says the two sides of the junta have kissed and made up, for some reason. So now the general's free to operate in the field the good old-fashioned way. I'm betting on beefed-up border guards after a demonstration of force and a few polite bows for the local newspapers. Now that it's safe for him to turn his back on his regular officers, what'll you bet the general means to take full credit for what we just pulled off for him?''

Gaston shrugged and said, "No bet. It's the way of the world, my child. The brass of bigness always takes the credit after the guns are no longer making the boom-boom. Is there some point to this discussion? A pretty widow, here in town, tells me she admires older men.''

"I wish you'd sober up and pay attention, dammit. We've still got our civilian duds in our packs. Have you counted the cash in those money belts you picked up yet?''

Gaston patted his middle and said, "Oui; it's all around my own adorable tummy at the moment. Caballero Blanco must have found the bandit business very rewarding lately. He alone was carrying over a thousand, U.S., in Mexican gold eagles, when someone put a sudden end to his profitable career. The others were funded more modestly, of course, but between them I was able to salvage close to another thousand. Why are we discussing money at a time like this, Dick? The widow said nothing about my paying her, and the food and drink seems to be free here.''

Captain Gringo said, "Pay attention, you drunk and horny little basser. I've been reading between the lines of this wire and I don't like the hidden message much. Read what the bottom line says. Never mind, I'd better read it for you. It says we're to stay here in San Lorenzo and wait for the general's main column. I mean, that's an *order*, not a suggestion."

"So what? I'm in no hurry to go anywhere tonight. Maybe the widow has a friend for you, hein?"

Captain Gringo studied his obliviously drunk and happy smaller comrade for a time. Then he nodded to himself and threw the balled-up telegram away, saying, "I've a better idea. Let's have a real orgy."

Gaston laughed and cackled, "Oui, mais where, and avec whom? I love you like a son, but you are not my type. Too tall, for one thing."

Captain Gringo laughed, stood up, and hauled Gaston to his own feet as he said, "I've got the dames lined up, over by the river landing. Are you up to skinny-dipping in the moonlight with more than one oversexed dame, Gaston?"

"Lead on. It sounds like an interesting challenge!"

So Captain Gringo led him through the crowd to the other side of the square. They were just moving into a dark side lane when Teresa caught up with them and asked where they were going. Captain Gringo said, "Private conversation about that plot you reported to me, Querida. Go back and save me a place at the buffet."

As soon as he and Gaston were alone again, the Frenchman belched and asked, "Why couldn't that one come to the orgy, Dick? She was built like the shithouse of bricks."

"The stuff we're going to meet is built better. Keep walking."

"Mais oui, don't let me fall at a time like *this!*"

He didn't. He led Gaston to the river's edge, moved down the bank into a clump of gumbo-limbo, and knocked Gaston cold with a sucker punch. Then he lowered his unconscious little pal gently to the ground and moved fast indeed in the next few minutes.

So, when Gaston came to, less than an hour later, they were drifting down the river in the moonlight and a stolen canoe, with the packs from their abandoned mules between them.

Gaston sat up, rubbing the side of his jaw thoughtfully, to ask, "Dick, why did you just coldcock a poor old man for no reason?"

Captain Gringo growled, "I didn't just coldcock you. It was quite a while ago, and I had a reason. You were wasting time arguing and we didn't have much time. I want to be at least a full day's march away when that fucking general shows up with a whole fucking division. He could probably lick us with a regiment, anyway. My new adelita tells me some of our own guys are having second thoughts about outsiders getting credit for a victory they want the history books to credit the Guatemalan army with, exclusively."

Gaston, more sober now, nodded and said, "Oh, thank you for knocking me out, Dick. That widow back there was pretty, but not pretty enough to spend one's last night alive with."

Captain Gringo saw little point in restating the obvious, so they drifted on awhile in silence before Gaston pulled himself up to a more comfortable position, stared out at the moonlit water all around, and observed, "I see your plan. This species of stream will carry us down to the British Honduran seaport of Belize, where, with civilian clothes and our handsome pale faces, we may pass for British beach bums long enough to hop a freighter."

He thought and added, "Eh bien, I know a very understanding whore with a heart of gold in Belize. But this line of retreat still strikes me as a très dangerous one, Dick. Do you know for a fact the general planned to rob us of our lives as well as credit for . . . What in the hell did we just do, Dick?"

Captain Gringo shrugged and said, "Whatever it was, the invasions are off until at least the next dry season, and, yeah, it's a safe bet the general intends to take full credit for it. I *don't* know, for sure, whether he'd be ruthless enough to pay us off with lead instead of gold. But he struck me as a tough old bird, and lead's a lot cheaper than gold. Dead men don't contradict official press releases much, either. Meanwhile, we're money ahead, we're still alive, so why take chances?"

He picked up a paddle from the bottom of the canoe and got to work decreasing the distance between them and the border as he added, "He can't pay us off, either way, once we're in British Honduras."

Gaston said, "True, but are the British constabulary really apt to go out of their way to make us feel welcome, all things considered?"

"Hell, Gaston, even if they know we led that confusion to the north, why would they be expecting us to paddle right into their Crown Colony? Do we look *that* stupid?"

Gaston laughed and said, "Mais non; if we had the brains of gnats we would of course be paddling the other way. And if our jolly general brags enough, they'll be more worried about a division of Guatemalans than a pair of innocent travelers. Is there another paddle in this species of soggy lumber?"

"Yeah, but wait 'til you're sober. I'm having enough trouble steering. Tell me about this lady you know in Belize, Gaston. Do you think she might have a friend?"

"I'm not going to tell you. The last time we discussed an orgy, you hit me in the head!"

Masterpieces
by Norman Mailer

__ANCIENT EVENINGS   *(A32-109, $4.95, U.S.A.)*
(A32-110, $5.95, Canada)

Set against the seductive beauty and languorous mystery of ancient Egypt, Norman Mailer's extraordinary narrative abounds with eroticism, magic and intrigue. More than ten years in the writing, ANCIENT EVENINGS is more than good fiction. It is the publishing event of 1983, and one of the great books of our time.

__THE EXECUTIONER'S SONG
(A36-353, $4.95, U.S.A.)
(A30-646, $5.95, Canada)

The execution is what the public remembers: on January 17, 1977, a firing squad at Utah State Prison put an end to the life of convicted murderer Gary Gilmore. But by then the real story was over—the true tale of violence and fear, jealousy and loss, of a love that was defiant even in death. Winner of the Pulitzer Prize. "The big book no one but Mailer could have dared . . . an absolutely astonishing book." —Joan Didion, *New York Times Book Review.*

To order, use the coupon below. If you prefer to use your own stationery, please include complete title as well as book number and price. Allow 4 weeks for delivery.

WARNER BOOKS
P.O. Box 690
New York, N.Y. 10019

Please send me the books I have checked. I enclose a check or money order (not cash), plus 50¢ per order and 50¢ per copy to cover postage and handling.*

_____ Please send me your free mail order catalog. (If ordering only the catalog, include a large self-addressed, stamped envelope.)

Name _____

Address _____

City _____

State _____ Zip _____

*N.Y. State and California residents add applicable sales tax.   98

The Best of Adventure
by RAMSAY THORNE